**Connie swallowed hard and bit down on her bottom lip, something she did whenever she was uncomfortable.**

"We made eye contact, but only for a second or maybe two. Then just as quick, one of the other men pulled him out the door."

"Damn, Connie. That means he might be able to identify you, too."

"No." She shook her head vehemently. "I don't think so. It was just a split second. Trace, everything happened so fast. There's no way he could've gotten a good look at me. Besides, he doesn't know who I am," she said in a rush, sounding as if she was trying to convince herself. "He knows nothing about me, and the FBI agent assured me that what I shared with them and my identity will be kept confidential."

Worry wound through Trace as he watched her carefully, noticing how agitated she was getting. He reached over and massaged the back of her neck.

"If you believe that, then why are you trembling?"

\* \* \*

Dear Reader,

After introducing Connie Shaw in *Sin City Temptation* (Harlequin Kimani Romance), I just had to give her a story!

In *His to Protect*, Connie is sweet, spunky, and her friends love her to death, but she has trust issues when it comes to men. Except there's one, Trace Halstead, who breaks through the barrier she's placed around her heart. She tries to ignore their attraction, but he's impossible to ignore, and when Connie's life is in jeopardy, Trace is the man who will protect her at all costs.

Journey with them as they both learn how to leave their troubled pasts behind and open their hearts to love again.

Enjoy!

*Sharon C. Cooper*

# HIS TO PROTECT

---

## Sharon C. Cooper

HARLEQUIN

ROMANTIC
SUSPENSE

# HARLEQUIN®
# ROMANTIC SUSPENSE™

Recycling programs
for this product may
not exist in your area.

ISBN-13: 978-1-335-62892-3

His to Protect

Copyright © 2021 by Sharon C. Cooper

All rights reserved. No part of this book may be used or reproduced in
any manner whatsoever without written permission except in the case of
brief quotations embodied in critical articles and reviews.

This is a work of fiction. Names, characters, places and incidents
are either the product of the author's imagination or are used fictitiously.
Any resemblance to actual persons, living or dead, businesses,
companies, events or locales is entirely coincidental.

This edition published by arrangement with Harlequin Books S.A.

For questions and comments about the quality of this book,
please contact us at CustomerService@Harlequin.com.

Harlequin Enterprises ULC
22 Adelaide St. West, 40th Floor
Toronto, Ontario M5H 4E3, Canada
www.Harlequin.com

Printed in U.S.A.

Award-winning and bestselling author of over thirty books **Sharon C. Cooper** writes contemporary romance as well as romantic suspense. She's been nominated for numerous awards and is the recipient of Romance Slam Jam Emma Awards for Author of the Year 2019, Favorite Hero 2019 (*Indebted*) and Romantic Suspense of the Year 2015 (*Truth or Consequences*), to name a few. When Sharon isn't writing, she's hanging out with her amazing husband, doing volunteer work or reading a good book (a romance, of course). To read more about Sharon and her novels, visit www.sharoncooper.net.

### Books by Sharon C. Cooper

### Harlequin Romantic Suspense

*His to Protect*

### Harlequin Kimani Romance

*Legal Seduction*
*Sin City Temptation*
*A Dose of Passion*
*Model Attraction*

Visit the Author Profile page at Harlequin.com for more titles.

For Al, the love of my life and the inspiration behind every hero I create—I adore you!

## Acknowledgments

Claire, Brenda and Yolanda,
you ladies are priceless! Love you!

To my amazing readers: I do this for you!
Thank you for always supporting my work!

# *Chapter 1*

*I thought mobile apps were supposed to make life easier.*

Constance Shaw growled under her breath when another message popped up on her cell-phone screen.

Your deposit could not be completed. Please try again later.

"Seriously? This is ridiculous."

"Talking to your phone is not going to change the results."

Connie glanced up to find her best friend, who also happened to be her boss, standing in the office doorway. "Fierce, fashionable and in charge" was the best way to describe Trinity Layton-Brooks, a former police officer who now owned a security firm, Layton Executive Protection Agency (LEPA).

Connie dropped down in her leather chair and tossed the phone on the desk. "I hate mobile apps. Looks like I'll be going to the bank at lunchtime."

Trinity strolled into the office. "Girl, don't get me started on anything technology-related."

Connie smiled when her friend got closer. "You have to be the *hottest* pregnant boss-lady on the planet. You're glowing."

Trinity was four months pregnant, and though Connie was thrilled for her best friend, she couldn't help but wonder when it would be her time. She absolutely loved her job as VP of Operations, but her personal life was lacking. Unlike Trinity, Connie didn't have the amazing husband, one-point-five kids and a life that fairy tales were made of. All the things that she someday wanted.

Trinity smiled and waved her off. "Oh, please. With only three hours of sleep, it's amazing I can even think straight. The glow you're seeing is probably perspiration from me sweating over that proposal for the state of Nevada. It's more involved than I thought."

"I know, right? I had a few late nights this week trying to pull together all of the requested information. I'm hoping to be finished with my part before I head to lunch today."

"Good. Then all that's left is for me to get my portion done."

Layton Executive Protection Agency provided personal protection to a high-end clientele, and Trinity was always looking for opportunities to expand their services. And as the VP of Operations, Connie's only concern lately had been making sure they stayed on top and kept up with demand. Business was great, and in only five years she had worked hard to help it become a million-dollar agency. They dominated the personal-security industry in Las Vegas and in Los Angeles. It helped that the extensive training and credentials of their security personnel were second to none.

Trinity sat in one of the gray upholstered guest chairs in front of Connie's desk and crossed her legs. "Kya Rae is becoming a problem, and we have to pull Trace off of her detail."

*Trace.*

*Trace Halstead.*

Just hearing the man's name sent fiery tingles scurrying over Connie's skin. Thinking of him in a professional capacity hadn't been working lately. Memories of their passionate night together blasted through her mind and sent heat propelling to every nerve in her body.

A month ago, after a work event, Connie had invited Trace, who was one of LEPA's security specialists, back to her place for a drink. She knew it probably wasn't the best idea to mix business with pleasure, but they'd been skirting around each other for months. Flirting and harmless banter had been their way of getting to know each other. What she hadn't counted on that evening was that the attraction between them would boil over.

She couldn't even blame her indiscretion on having too much to drink, because she hadn't. One glass of Moscato, a tad bit of curiosity and a huge dose of mutual sexual attraction had pulled them together like a neodymium magnet. One night. That was all it took for Trace Halstead to ruin her for any other man. There was no way anyone else existed who could pleasure her body as thoroughly as he had.

For that reason alone, Connie could almost forget that he was a pain in the butt. Maybe not all the time, but often enough to make her occasionally want to strangle his fine self. Too bad she liked him. A lot. LEPA might not have a no-fraternizing policy, but Connie had her own set of rules. The one at the top of the list: never get romantically involved with a coworker again, especially a subordinate.

Been there.

Done that.

It didn't end well.

So much for rules, though. That one had imploded when she hooked up with Trace. And it turned out to be one of the most exciting, mind-blowing missteps Connie had ever made. Now, each time his name was mentioned or he was in her presence, her mind took her back to the night that he had thrown her world off-kilter.

Connie leaned back in her desk chair and inhaled deeply. Then, releasing a slow, cleansing breath, she brought her thoughts back to the present, willing her libido back under control.

"Hmm…interesting," Trinity said, studying her as if Connie had just shared a theory on how to make underwire bras more comfortable. "I mention Trace and your whole face lit up. I think I even see your cheeks tinting. What's that all about? What haven't you told me?"

Connie glanced down and brushed invisible lint off

her black pants as she concentrated on schooling her expression. "First of all, I don't blush."

Her skin tone was fairer than Trinity's, but still dark enough that a blush wouldn't show. She couldn't deny that her musings had sent warmth spreading through her body. Of course, Trinity *would* notice. Her friend had always been observant, and getting anything past her was almost impossible. Which was why she'd been an excellent police officer.

Connie slid a lock of hair behind her ear and straightened her shoulders. "Secondly, don't look for something that isn't there. Trace and I are coworkers. I might even go as far as calling him a friend, but that's it. Nothing else."

Her words were spoken with finality, and Connie believed them herself. For the most part.

A slow smile spread across Trinity's mouth. "Mmm-hmm. You keep telling yourself that, but I know better. I'll just sit back and continue enjoying the show of you two pretending that there's nothing going on between you. But for now, let's get back to *Trace's* situation. Who's available that we can replace him with?"

"You know he's scheduled to be on Kya's detail for another two weeks. At least until after the music festival."

"I know, but Trace said he can't do it. He didn't give details about what she did, but he said the woman is getting bolder and more aggressive with her advances. It's making him uncomfortable. We can't have that. She must've really stepped over the line if he's asking to be reassigned."

"What about Riley? Did Kya come on to him, too?" Connie asked of the other security specialist on the assignment.

Trinity yawned noisily and quickly covered her mouth with the back of her hand. "Oh, man. Sorry about that. I think the lack of sleep is catching up to me. And, no, Riley said she's irritating, but she hasn't made him uncomfortable. Just Trace."

This wasn't the first time Kya had made a pass at Trace. She'd been a client off and on for eight months. Each time she needed personal protection she requested a two-men detail. Trace was always one of them.

He was one of the agency's most requested guards, especially by women between the ages of twenty-five and fifty. Connie couldn't much blame their female clients for falling for him. Trace was not only tall, dark and *fine*, but he was also smart, funny and charismatic. And as a former US Navy officer, he had the whole alpha, top-dog persona nailed down.

Even still, that didn't give any client the right to proposition him, or make him uncomfortable with unwanted advances.

"I'll look into the situation and identify someone to take his place." Connie turned to her laptop and pulled up their personnel database. "Does Kya know that she's losing Trace?"

"Not yet. I told him to give us an hour. We need to see who's been assigned to her in the past that Kya will approve of before he tells her."

"You know she's not going to let him go without an argument."

"I agree. That's why I want you to talk to her."

Connie jerked her head away from the computer screen and narrowed her eyes at her friend. "Why me? Why can't you do it?"

"Because you have more tact than I do, and you care about keeping her as a client."

Connie laughed. "You do, too."

"I do…to a point. Yes, Kya has sent us a ton of business, but her inappropriate behavior is unacceptable. It was bad enough that time when she thought it was okay to prance around her house naked in front of our guys. She didn't care that she made them uncomfortable. When Trace suggested they give her privacy, she demanded they stay put. Don't even get me started on how many times she's propositioned Trace. He hasn't accused her of sexual harassment, but technically… We need to face it—she's a problem. With all of that said, the news should come from you since she's afraid of you."

"Oh, please. That girl is not afraid of me."

"Uh, *yeah*, she is. Remember that time when she requested our guys to escort her to court? Then when they did, she started a fight with that news cameraman and expected Noah to fight her battle. I'll never forget when you cursed her out."

Connie's mouth dropped open. "Really, Trinity? How can you even say that with a straight face? You know good and well I didn't curse that woman out."

"Okay, maybe not, but you have the amazing ability to curse someone out without using a swear word."

"I didn't exactly tell her off. I just made it clear that

if she couldn't carry herself like an adult and a lady when our people are with her, she'd have to find another agency."

"Well, whatever you said worked. Now you need to talk to her about Trace. This is the second time she's made a pass at him. She doesn't get another chance."

A knock sounded on Connie's office door.

"Come in," she called out.

The door slid open. "Connie, have you seen…? Oh, Trinity, you're in here. I was looking for you. Your husband's on line one," Jade, their executive assistant, said.

"Okay, thanks. I'll pick it up in my office. Tell him to give me a second."

"Will do," Jade said, backing out of the office and closing the door behind her.

Trinity stood. "Okay, so we agree that you'll save Trace from Kya?"

Connie gave an exaggerated sigh. "*Fine.* If I must."

Trinity grinned. "Don't act like you ain't happy to get him away from that woman. I know you want him all to your—"

"Don't go there. He and I are just friends and co-workers. If this is one of your attempts to push us together, forget it."

Honestly, Connie was more than happy to assign someone else to Kya's detail. She hated the idea of any woman coming on to Trace. Not because she wanted him for herself, but… Heck, who was she kidding? She totally wanted him, but she had no intention of admitting that to her friend or anyone else.

"I don't know why you keep fighting the inevitable. You and Trae-Trae would be perfect together."

"You know he hates when you call him that."

Trinity and Trace had grown up in the same neighborhood as kids and had always had a brother-sister-like relationship. After he left the navy and moved back to Las Vegas, he joined LEPA and had been with the agency ever since. He and Connie had only met a year ago, when she relocated to the Vegas office from their branch in Los Angeles.

Connie was staying firm to keeping her and Trace as friends. Especially since every time she opened her heart to someone, they found a way to disappoint her. Or maybe it was that she just chose wrong when it came to men. Either way, she was good at cutting her losses and moving on. She didn't want that to happen with Trace, though. If they didn't complicate whatever was happening between them, they could at least stay friends.

"Oh." Trinity snapped her fingers. "On a serious note. What do you think about him in a management role? We're going to need to set up another team, specifically when some of these contracts start rolling in. I don't want to oversee another group, and I know you don't. Instead of hiring someone from the outside, how about we promote from within?"

Connie had actually thought about that months ago, when Trace had filled in for one of the other managers. He had phenomenal people skills, was dependable and well respected at the company. Besides that, he knew how Trinity and Connie liked things run. A frisson of anticipation coursed through her at the prospect of seeing his handsome face in the office every day. His presence always made her feel giddy inside. Then again, if she wanted to maintain some type of professionalism, having Trace around all the time could prove challenging.

"I think it's an excellent idea to promote from within. I just don't think Trace will want an office job. He likes to be out and about, and a part of the action. Sitting at a desk all day will bore him to death."

Trinity nodded. "You're probably right. Okay, I'm outta here. Let me know how it goes with Kya."

"Will do. Oh, and I'm going to the bank during my lunch break and probably stop at the sandwich shop on my way back. Want anything?"

"Yeah, my usual, but make sure they don't put onions on the salad or the sandwich." She placed her hand on her small baby bump. "This kid always gives me trouble after I eat onions."

"Got it. No onions."

Three hours later, Connie strolled into the bank. The old, run-down building was one brick away from crumbling into a heap, but at least the air conditioner worked. The cool air kissed her heated skin, and she soaked it up. Deciding to walk to the bank from the office might not have been the best decision. Her silk blouse stuck to her as if glued to her skin. It was only April and already the Vegas temperature had hit eighty degrees.

Connie removed her sunglasses and blinked several times, giving her eyes time to adjust to the fluorescent lights. Clearly, she hadn't been the only person to decide to drop by during the lunch hour. A couple of people sat talking to personal bankers, while at least four others stood in line for a teller.

Connie couldn't remember the last time she'd been inside the bank. She headed to the line, her heels clicking on the ceramic tiles. The sound echoed off the walls.

"Next," one of the tellers called out.

While standing in line, Connie pulled out her cell phone to check emails. A smile kicked up the corners of her mouth as she skimmed the email from Trinity, letting her know about a meeting later. She especially liked the last part of the message.

All hail to the queen of getting stuff done. Kya's been handled, and you managed to finish your portion of the state application. When I grow up, I want to be like you.

Connie snorted. She and Trinity had met their junior year of high school, and from day one Connie recognized her friend's ambition. Trinity had that never-say-quit attitude and went after everything she wanted. If anything, Connie wanted to be more like her. Maybe not so much a business owner, but she'd love to be married with children one day. But that was never going to happen if she refused to trust any more men with her heart.

"Next."

Connie glanced up to see that the three people who were in line were now in front of tellers. Four others had filed into line behind her.

"Good afternoon," the bank teller said when Connie approached. "Thanks for your patience. How may I help you today?"

"Hi. I just want to make a deposit. I tried using the mobile app, but for the last two days, it wouldn't let me deposit checks."

"I'm sorry about that," the woman said as she processed the deposit. "A few others have had problems with the app and the bank is looking into the issue."

Connie nodded. Computers were great when they worked. But when they didn't, they were a pain in the butt.

"Okay, you're all set, Ms. Shaw. Is there anything else I can help you with?"

"Nope, that's it. Thank you."

Connie went in the opposite direction of the entrance and around the line, hoping to run into Richard Holmes. He was the loan officer who'd been instrumental in getting her a good rate on a mortgage when she first moved to town. She didn't visit the bank often, but when she did, she always made a point to stop and say hello to him.

Connie peeked into his office, glad to see he wasn't with anyone. When he glanced up from the document he was reading, she smiled and gave a little wave.

"Well, hello, stranger," he greeted her.

He removed his reading glasses and set them on the desk before approaching her. In his early sixties, Richard Holmes had kind green eyes that crinkled in the corners whenever he smiled, the way he was doing now. His full head of hair was grayer than she remembered, but he still had a pep in his step as he approached her.

"You didn't have to stop what you were doing," Connie said as he shook her hand. "I just wanted to say hello on my way out."

"I'm glad you did. I needed to get up and stretch these old bones, anyway." He laughed, the sound deep and hearty like Santa Claus giving an enthusiastic *ho-ho-ho*. "How's that house treating you?" he asked, and they slowly walked toward the entrance.

"It's great, but I'm thinking about getting something bigger." The two-bedroom, one-and-a-half-bathroom 1970s bungalow was a cute starter home, but Connie was ready for something bigger and more modern.

"Well, make sure you stop by and see me when you're ready. Interest rates are low and it's a good time to buy."

"You'll be the first person I call. Have you—?"

"Hands in the air!"

Connie startled at the sudden booming voice and tightened the hold on her purse strap. She stood frozen in place, shocked to see a masked man a few feet away, holding a gun. It was then she noticed two additional men, dressed similarly in all black. One was standing on top of the counter overlooking the tellers and was waving his gun around. The other was pointing his own weapon at those in line.

"Get those hands up and get on the ground!" the robber closest to her yelled. His menacing voice sent chills scurrying down Connie's spine. "Move it. Now! I'd better see everybody's hands."

Ice clogged Connie's veins. She shook with fear as she and the others were forced to lie facedown on the floor. The erratic rhythm of her heartbeat thumped hard and fast, loud enough that others in the room could probably hear it.

Where the hell were the cops? Or even the security guard that she'd seen when she first arrived? The building was old, but surely it had some type of alarm system.

Mind racing like a jet-engine supercar, Connie was lying on her stomach, her arms out where they could be easily seen. Cold from the tiled floor seeped through her thin blouse and pants, but it did nothing to tamp down the fear spreading through her body like a wildfire.

The whole scenario was playing out like a bad dream as the thieves yelled instructions to the tellers, rushing them to stuff money into their bags. Connie had never felt so helpless in all of her life. Somebody needed to do *something*.

Through lowered lashes, she peeped out at the gunman who had been the closest. He swept his gun back and forth anxiously, while his partners gathered money from the tellers.

"Hurry up. We have three minutes," one of them roared to the other two.

Movement to Connie's left caught her attention. Richard, who'd been lying an arm's length from her moments ago, was doing a very slow belly crawl backward toward his office. He was barely moving, but if she noticed him, the robbers might, too.

Connie wanted to scream at him to stop. What was he thinking? These guys had weapons and looked as if they meant business. Before she could think her next thought, one of the masked men roughly yanked Richard up by the back of his collar.

Connie screamed, and she slapped her own hand over her mouth. Heart racing and throat tightening, she quickly turned her head and slammed her eyes closed. Panic rocketed through her body. Curling into a ball with her arms covering her head, she tried making herself appear as small as possible.

*Please don't let them come over here. Please, please, please...* Her pulse pounded in her ears like a locomotive roaring down the track as she lay frozen with fear.

"So you want to be a tough guy, huh?" the gunman growled.

A scuffle broke out. Richard cried and howled in pain as the sound of fists hitting skin pierced the air. Tears filled Connie's eyes. She felt so helpless, and her heart broke as he pleaded with his attacker.

Two gunshots, thundering like fireworks, echoed through the air.

Connie could hear her screams mingling with the others in the room, and her heart stopped when a loud thump rattled the floor.

*Oh, no... Richard.*

"Dammit! What have you done?" one of the robbers yelled. "We gotta get out of here. Hurry! Go! Go! Go!"

Loud footsteps echoed by Connie's head. She lifted her face from the protective barrier of her arms and chanced a glance just as the last man reached the main door. He started removing his mask but stopped...and turned.

Startling gray eyes met hers.

Held.

One second...then two... Then he was gone.

The breath Connie hadn't realized she was holding whooshed through her mouth, and her body went limp.

*Oh. Dear. God.*

# Chapter 2

The moment Trace climbed into his Chevy Camaro, he yanked his tie back and forth with more force than needed to loosen the knot. Anger vibrated deep inside him at the crap that Kya tried to pull.

How the hell did he end up in situations like that? Did he have some damn sign on his forehead that said Feel Free to Touch Me at Will? Had he been the one to touch her inappropriately, his ass would've been hauled off to jail. It was bad enough months ago, when she walked around naked in front of him and his team member, but this time she had crossed the line.

*Just let it go, man*, he told himself and tossed the black tie into the passenger seat. But that was easier said than done. Even after he'd started his car and it roared to life, his mind kept going back to Kya's little stunt. He hadn't been able to get away from the woman fast enough, and he was using the word *woman* loosely. The A-list pop star was only twenty-two. A child, in his book.

Still, she had to know better than to grab a grown man's *package* without permission. But what if his reaction had been different? What if he had accidentally hit her in the process of getting out of her grasp? He had instinctively, and roughly, grabbed her wrist and pushed her away, practically knocking her down without thinking. It had been a knee-jerk reaction, and what angered him more was that she, apparently, had thought it was funny.

Trace shook his head, not even wanting to think about how the situation could've easily spiraled out of control. Lucky for him Riley had been there to witness the incident. The other thing that gave Trace a little peace was knowing that Connie had just terminated Kya's account with LEPA. He would never have to worry about getting assigned to her detail again since she wouldn't be able to hire their services in Las Vegas or at their Los Angeles location.

Trace hadn't meant for the situation to result in a lost contract. He knew the company would lose a substantial amount of money. He mainly just wanted to be removed from Kya's detail. But Connie insisted that terminating the agreement was protecting both him and the company, especially since Kya refused to have female guards. She would never be able to put their team in a compromising position in the future.

Connie had come through again.

Trace felt the tension in his shoulders start to ease and a slow smile spread across his face. His spitfire supervisor might be small in stature, but she carried herself like a badass boss. She didn't take crap from anybody. Something he more than respected.

Lately, it was hard to think of her without remembering that amazing night they shared. Trace had been secretly in lust with Connie since the first time they'd met a year ago. Their friendship over the last few months had blossomed into something much more than boss and direct report. At least for him. Connie, though? Not so much. After their passionate night together, she mentioned they could be friends but never anything more. Yet the attraction between them? Too intense to ignore.

He was so into Connie that if it meant him changing careers to be with her, he'd do it. The timing was good. He and one of his brothers had been planning to open a private investigation firm. Langston currently worked for the FBI, but like Trace, he was ready for a change in his life. The Halsteads were problem solvers by nature, and with his US Navy background, and Langston's law-enforcement experience, they'd always be prepared if a case went sideways. Besides that, Trace's business degree, which he'd earned while in the navy, was going to pay off for them in a big way.

His cell phone rang, and Sylvia's telephone number popped up on the car's dashboard screen. They'd dated off and on for a couple of years, but he had ended things with her after his passionate night with Connie. He knew then that he wanted to pursue an intimate relationship with his boss, even if she claimed they couldn't get seriously involved.

Instead of ignoring the call, which was his first instinct, he answered with the car's Bluetooth. "Hello."

"Hey, baby. I've been thinking about you," Sylvia crooned, her voice echoing through the speakers.

"How's it going, Sylvia?"

"It would be going better if you weren't avoiding me. How about dinner tonight at my place?"

"Sylvia, we've already talked about this," Trace said as he stopped at a traffic light. "You're a nice lady, but I can't see you anymore."

She was beautiful and intelligent, and they got along great. But Trace just couldn't see a future with her. Actually, he hadn't considered settling down with any of the women he'd been with. It didn't matter that he was still single at thirty-four. None of them made him want to give up his bachelor card.

But then Connie had come along. Everything about the woman, from her sassiness to her sharp mind and sexy body, turned him on. He wanted nothing more than to take their friendship and turn it into something more. She was the *only* woman he could actually envision having a future with. That probably should've scared him, since it was a first.

Since realizing that he wanted more with Connie, he'd been turning down any invites from other women. So far Sylvia was the only one who couldn't seem to move on. She called once or twice a week, and with each conversation, Trace made it clear that they could no longer see each other. Yet she continued.

Trace's cell phone signaled another call coming in. *Trinity.*

"Sylvia, I have to go. Take care of yourself." He disconnected, not giving her a chance to respond, then answered the other line. "I was just heading into the office. I hope you're not calling to tell me I have to go back to Kya's," he said by way of a greeting.

"No, actually, I'm calling about Connie." The seriousness in her tone had Trace holding the steering wheel tighter.

"What's going on?"

"The bank up the street was robbed this afternoon. Connie was there."

Trace's heart slammed against his chest. "What? Is she…is she okay? Was she hurt? Was anyone hurt?" The rapid-fire questions flowing from his mouth only amplified the anxiety suddenly building inside him. She had to be all right.

"As far as I know, physically Connie is fine. A security guard was hurt, and it sounds like he'll be okay. But a loan officer was shot and is in serious condition."

"But Connie's okay?" Trace asked again, wanting to make sure.

"Yes, as far as I know," she said in exasperation. "But I haven't talked to her. Max just called and said that she was giving a statement at the police station. He wasn't sure if Connie had called me and wanted to give me a heads-up of where she was," Trinity said. Maxwell Layton was a police sergeant with the Las Vegas Police Department.

Trace's chest tightened with trepidation as his

thoughts ran rampant while he sped toward the highway that would take him to the office. "Did Connie
call you?"

"No. I texted her earlier when she didn't return to
the office after lunch. She responded by text, but all she
said was 'I'm okay. Will explain later.'"

"Well, that's a good sign. She's all right." He gripped
the steering wheel tighter as those three words volleyed
inside his mind, willing them to be true. She had to be
okay. Trace wouldn't rest until he knew she was physically and mentally fine.

"I hope you're right. I just never know with Connie.
The woman could be seriously hurt and still say she's
fine. That happened once when we were in college and
a brawl broke out in the dining hall. Connie had nothing to do with the fight, but got caught in the middle of
it and ended up getting trampled. We knew she'd been
banged up, but she didn't mention that she was in pain.
It wasn't until the next day that we realized she had
several fractured ribs. She'll never admit if she's hurt."

Trace hadn't heard that story, but from what he knew
of Connie, he could totally see her putting on a brave
front. She always made it seem as if she could handle
anything.

"I'm not sure why she's at the police station," Trinity continued. "When I was a cop, in cases like this,
we'd do the questioning on-site. So something's up. Max
doesn't have all the details, but he said he'd look into it
and get back to me."

Trace didn't want to wait. He'd rather hear directly

from Connie about what had happened. He'd call her as soon as he got off the phone with Trinity.

"I hate to ask you this, Trace, but can you go to the police station to meet her? Connie's going to need a ride since she walked to the bank, and I was thinking—"

"I'm on it," Trace said quickly. "I assume she's at the precinct Max works out of?"

"Yes…and thanks for doing this."

She already knew that there wasn't anything he wouldn't do for her or Connie. Not just because he worked for them, but because they were a part of him. Trinity, one of his best friends, and Connie… Well, he wasn't exactly sure what category to put Connie in at the moment.

A short while later, Trace entered the police station. Once he was through security, he trotted up three stairs and glanced around, hearing muffled voices to his left and right from behind closed doors. In front of him was a long desk counter where two uniformed officers were working.

"Trace."

He whipped around and saw Maxwell, dressed in his blue uniform, walking toward him.

"Hey, man. I was hoping to run into you," Trace said in a rush, his heart rate elevated. He had broken every speed limit, cutting his arrival time in half, in an effort to get to Connie and see for himself that she was fine.

They shook hands and pulled each other into a one-armed hug. Trace hadn't seen Max in months.

Growing up, he and his brothers used to hang out

with Maxwell since they lived in the same neighborhood. Unlike Trace, who'd joined the navy, his two older brothers and Maxwell had gone into law enforcement.

"It's good seeing you. I just hate it's under these circumstances," Maxwell said.

"I agree. Where is she?"

"Follow me. I was looking out for you since Trinity told me you were on your way."

Trace walked alongside Maxwell and followed him through the door to the right of the desk counter. Then they entered a hallway with a few offices with glass walls.

Maxwell slowed. "Connie's fine, but she's a little shaken up. You know she's like a sister to me. I hate she was even there. While one of the responding officers questioned her, they realized that she got a partial ID on one of the robbers. That's why she was asked to come to the sta—"

"Wait. What?" Unease clawed at Trace. "She recognized one of them?"

An officer peeked out from behind a closed door. "Hey, Sarge. You got a minute?" he said to Maxwell.

"Yeah, give me a second. I'll be right there." Maxwell turned back to Trace. "The bank robbery is under the Feds' jurisdiction. So they'll be handling the case from here. Connie will be working with them, but right now she's with our sketch artist."

Trace hated the idea of Connie being anywhere near this case. It was bad enough she'd had to experience a bank robbery. "What do you mean, *working with them*?

The Feds aren't planning to use her to draw the robbers out, are they?"

Maxwell glanced around as if making sure no one was nearby before leaning close to Trace. "I'm sure they'll have more questions for her. There's been three bank robberies in the area within a four-month time frame. We think they're related. So far, Connie is the only witness we have who got a clear look at one of the robbers. She's the only one who's been able to give anything helpful so far."

Trace shook his head. "Nah, man. It's too dangerous. I get them needing her to answer questions and help with the sketch, but that's it. They can't be using her as some type of bait. I'm not letting that happen," he said with conviction.

Connie wasn't his. Trace had no right to have a say in any part of her life. Yet, even as her friend, her well-being was important to him.

Maxwell gripped Trace's shoulder and squeezed. "I get it, man. I'm worried about her, too. She's like a sister to me. But only a handful of us know she can partially identify one of the bank robbers. She won't be put in any danger. The Feds will probably check in with her over the next couple of days to see if she remembers anything else. But just so you know, Connie told them that she's willing to assist any way she can."

"What?"

Maxwell shrugged. "That's what she said. I can't see them needing her after today, though. Her working with a sketch artist is going to be very helpful. Oh, and is Langston still with the FBI?"

"Yeah, he's been undercover for the last few years. Now he's back and working out of the Vegas field office."

Maybe Trace could get some information from his brother, but he doubted it. Like most law-enforcement agents, Langston was tight-lipped about cases, even more so when it was someone else's.

Trace looked up when Connie and two other men exited a door. They were about thirty feet away. He couldn't hear what was being said, but he assumed the guys must be FBI, if their dark suits were any indication.

"She's going to be fine," Maxwell said.

Trace hoped he was right. He couldn't take his eyes off her. Her pink sleeveless blouse was wrinkled, something he assumed had to do with the bank robbery. Connie was normally meticulous about her appearance; there was no way she would be out in public looking disheveled. Even her dark pants had gray smudges, as if she'd been rolling around on a dusty floor. The black flats on her feet weren't her norm, either. At around five-five and petite, she rarely wore anything other than high heels at the office, at least as far as Trace had seen. Right now, though, she appeared almost timid. Or maybe that was what he wanted to see, so that she'd need him somehow.

How pitiful was he, that he was looking for any excuse to hold her close? Smart, confident and self-sufficient, based on what Trinity had told him about her, she probably wouldn't *want* to be coddled.

Connie folded her arms around her midsection in a protective move. As if sensing him watching, she turned her head slightly and their gazes collided. She pushed her long, dark curls behind her ear, allowing him a better view of her beautiful face. Her golden-brown skin glowed beneath the fluorescent lights, and she gave him a shy smile before returning her attention to the suits.

"I hate this," Trace mumbled under his breath.

"Hate what?"

"I hate that she's caught up in this mess." He wasn't sure how far she'd go to help the FBI, but if they asked her to do something in the name of helping them catch the bastards, she'd do it.

"You have to give her some credit, man," Maxwell said, as if reading his mind. "She might be tiny, but she's tough. She'll be all right."

Maxwell had known her longer than Trace. If he said she was tough enough, Trace would have to believe him. That didn't mean that he wouldn't be right there to step in if she needed him.

"Well, let me get back to work. Take care of our girl and holler if you need anything."

"Will do," Trace said, giving him a fist bump before Maxwell headed down the hallway.

When Trace turned back to Connie, she was walking toward him, her posture rigid, as if she was carrying the world on her shoulders. He watched her carefully, needing to see with his own eyes that she was all right. Physically, she appeared fine, but Trace didn't miss the way her gaze bounced around. She was running her hands up and down her bare arms, as if cold. The closer she got to him, the more agitated she seemed.

His heart rate kicked up when their gazes finally collided. He had never seen her look so vulnerable and so worn out as she did in that moment. The worst part was that he wasn't sure what to do for her.

"You all right?" he asked, knowing it was a dumb question, but it was all he could think to say.

Instead of speaking, Connie nodded and swallowed. Folding her bottom lip between her teeth, she gnawed on it as her features contorted into a mask of anguish. Tears suddenly filled her eyes. The sight was like taking a punch to the stomach. Trace could practically feel the mental and emotional battles taking place within her.

*Ah, hell.*

"Come here," he said, trying to keep his own warring emotions in check.

He opened his arms, and Connie practically fell into his embrace. Tightening his hold around her, Trace held her close as her shoulders shook and she silently cried against his chest.

He could only imagine what it had been like, being present during a bank robbery. What had she seen? Had the man who'd been shot been nearby? Then to have to recount the details, reliving the moments over and over, had probably taken a toll. He hated seeing her like this. Watching any woman cry was hard, but when that woman was Connie, his pint-size dynamo, it was even tougher. The thought of something or someone putting a dent in her strong, vibrant personality broke his heart.

So many thoughts and questions jockeyed inside his

head—questions he wanted answers to, but not yet. Right now, Connie just needed to know that he was there for her.

"It's going to be all right," he said close to her ear.

Minutes ticked by as they stood on the side of the hallway. He ignored the sidelong glances they were getting from officers and employees milling about. All that mattered at that moment was the woman in his arms.

Trace placed a kiss on top of her head, her mass of curls tickling his nose. Of course, he had dreamed of having her in his arms again, but not like this. Not when she was so upset.

As her sobs quieted, Connie slowly loosened her arms from around his waist. When she pulled back, she blotted her face with the heel of her hand and didn't meet his eyes right away.

"Sorry for crying all over you." She waved her hands around. "I just couldn't hold it in any longer."

Trace cupped her face between his hands, forcing her to look at him. He stared into her beautiful, but sad, hazel eyes. "What can I do?" he asked, brushing the pads of his thumbs over her wet cheeks.

Tears hung on her long lashes, and a wobbly smile lifted the corners of her mouth. "You being here is enough. Thank you for coming."

Trace nodded. He believed in fate, and being pulled from his assignment early had been perfect timing. He and Connie might not be a couple yet, but he already knew he wanted to be the man who came to her rescue.

"Always. I'll always come when you need me." His hands slid over her shoulders and down her arms as he took a good look at her. She looked okay, but he needed to know for sure. "Were you hurt?"

"No." She shook her head, still wiping her face. "It was just the scariest thing I've ever experienced."

"I'm sure it was. Come on. Let's get out of here." Trace draped his arm over her shoulder and guided her out of the building.

"Thanks for picking me up," Connie said when they were outside.

"No problem. I'm glad I was available."

He removed his arm from around her shoulder and grabbed hold of Connie's small hand. He half expected her to pull out of his grasp, but was glad when she gave him a little squeeze instead.

"I'm over here." He guided her across the parking lot and stopped at the black Camaro. "So what do you think?"

Her eyes grew large. "I didn't know you bought a new car. It's beautiful."

"Yeah, it was way past time for me to retire the Jeep." This new vehicle had been a gift to himself after the bonus he had received for his last assignment.

He helped her into the passenger side before climbing into the driver's seat.

"I knew you'd been talking about needing a new ride, but I didn't peg you as the sports-car type." She ran her hand over the dashboard as her gaze swept over the interior. "I think I'm in love with your car."

Trace laughed, wishing she was referring to him with the same awe in her voice. Instead of starting the vehicle, he glanced at her. "Are you sure you're all right? I know I keep asking, but—"

"I'm sure. I know I got a little emotional back there, but really, I'm good. I just hope they catch these guys. The thought of them still out there, possibly planning another robbery, pisses me off. Two people are in the hospital because of those assholes. Excuse my language, but I'm so…I'm so angry, especially knowing Richard is still in surgery."

"Richard?"

"Yeah, he was the loan officer I was talking to before the robbery. I heard him get shot."

Trace shook his head and started the car. "Senseless. Another senseless shooting."

During his years in the navy, his tours of duty had taken him to some rough countries. He had seen so much crap that he would never be able to unsee. Now, back on US soil, he still found it bugged the hell out of him to hear about crimes and killings that just didn't make sense.

"It's like people don't value life anymore," he said, but stopped himself before launching into one of his rants about foolishness. "I'm glad you're okay."

"I'm fine. I just don't know if I'll ever get that man's gray eyes out of my mind."

Trace turned to her. "Exactly what were you able to ID?"

"I saw his eyes and part of a tattoo on his neck."

"Did he see you?"

Connie swallowed hard and bit down on her bottom lip, something she did whenever she was uncomfortable. "We made eye contact, but only for a second or maybe two. Then, just as quick, one of the other men pulled him out the door."

"Damn, Connie. That means he might be able to identify you, too."

"No." She shook her head vehemently. "I don't think so. It was just a split second. Trace, everything happened so fast. There's no way he could've gotten a good look at me. Besides, he doesn't know who I am," she said in a rush, sounding as if she was trying to convince herself. "He knows nothing about me, and the FBI agent assured me that what I shared with them and my identity will be kept confidential."

Worry wound through Trace as he watched her carefully, noticing how agitated she was getting. He reached over and massaged the back of her neck.

"If you believe that, then why are you trembling?"

# Chapter 3

"Maybe because you have the air conditioner on full blast," Connie said, trying to lighten the moment. Trace wasn't laughing, though.

The last thing she wanted was to keep thinking about the robbery. She'd held herself together through the ordeal, while being questioned and even while she worked with the sketch artist. It hadn't been until she saw Trace and walked toward him that she'd felt her brave front slipping. Seeing the worry on his handsome face and the way he stared at her had loosened something inside her.

"It's like you're trying to freeze me to death," she persisted, trying again to ease the tension in the car. "Of course, I'm—"

"Sweetheart, quit deflecting and talk to me." His stoic

expression was almost intimidating, but Connie knew he was only concerned about her well-being.

Right now, though, she would prefer it if he flashed that crooked grin that made her knees weak. Or she wouldn't mind seeing his panty-dropping smile that always made her heart beat a little faster. He was such a gorgeous man, with smooth, sepia-toned skin, always flawlessly groomed with his hair cut low and his mustache and goatee perfectly trimmed. It was no wonder women practically threw themselves at him. He was *that* good-looking.

"Talk to me," he repeated.

"Adrenaline, Trace. Maybe I'm trembling because the adrenaline that was pumping through my veins a while ago is slowly slipping away. I'll admit, I'm a *little* nervous. This all seems unreal. One minute I'm making a deposit at the bank because the stupid app didn't work. The next thing I know, I'm facedown on the floor while masked men hold me and other people at gunpoint. I might not have seen my life flash before my eyes, but I thought I was going to die."

"Tell me what you told the cops."

Connie swallowed as the bank scene filled her mind. She told Trace everything that had happened before she and Richard had realized the bank was being robbed.

"You see stuff like that in the movies or on TV, but to experience it felt like I was living out a nightmare." Connie glanced out the windshield, watching as people walked in and out of the police station. "One robber was barking orders at the teller while the other two were making sure people didn't move. Richard moved."

Trace continued massaging the back of her neck, and Connie soaked up the comfort his hand provided. That, along with the heady scent of his cologne—a woodsy, citrus mix that surrounded her—was distracting. A good distraction, but a distraction nonetheless.

"What do you mean, he was moving?"

"Trace, can we just not talk about this right now?" The words flew from her mouth with more bite than intended, but she didn't want to keep reliving this.

"Moving where?" he asked as if she hadn't just asked him to drop it. "I need to know."

Connie huffed out a breath. "At first, Richard was on the floor to my left. Then it looked as if he was trying to ease back into his office. I'm not a hundred percent sure what he was up to. He was barely moving. I don't even know how the robber noticed. I felt Richard crawling before I actually saw him move. If that makes any sense. I'm not sure where the robber was standing, but he…" The words caught in her throat.

Connie tried focusing on how good the massage to her neck felt. She didn't want to be taken back to the sounds in the bank. She didn't want to relive those last moments of lying on the floor. More than anything, she didn't want to see Richard being yanked to his feet like a rag doll.

Tears pricked the backs of her eyes. *God, please let him be all right.*

"Tell me the rest," Trace said gently.

"Why? Why are you doing this?"

"Because someone other than the police, someone who has your back, should know what you saw, what you went through. I also want to know who or what type of people we're dealing with. We don't know if they're random thugs. Or if they are a part of organized crime or a gang. I trust law enforcement to a point. I know they are going to try and get these guys, but I *need* to know everything. I need to know if there's a chance that the perps, whoever they are, will come after you."

He spoke with such passion and determination. The conviction behind each word warmed her heart, and deep down, she knew Trace was a man she could count on.

His dark, assessing eyes searched hers, and before Connie knew it, tears trailed down her cheeks. She quickly swiped them away, but they fell faster. Harder. She couldn't keep up with them.

"This is ridiculous. I can't seem to stop crying. I *never* cry."

"Aww, sweetheart. It's not my intent to upset you," Trace said and pulled her into his arms.

It didn't matter that the center console was cutting into her side; she needed this hug. Needed to be held close. The moment between them wasn't sexually charged, like usual. Right now, he wasn't the man she secretly liked more than she cared to admit. No, this was her coworker offering her comfort. Her friend. Nothing else.

"I've never been so scared in all of my life," she mumbled against Trace's shoulder before pulling away.

He opened the center console, pulled out a travel-size pack of tissue and handed it to her. "I hate it that you

went through that, but I need to know what transpired
when they caught Richard moving."

"I actually screamed. I hurried and turned away,
hoping they wouldn't come over to where I was lying.
Then it sounded like the guy and Richard might've been
wrestling or something. I'm not totally sure. I didn't
see them. I could only hear the scuffle. Seconds later,
there were gunshots. I knew immediately, because it
sounded like the time Trinity took me to the gun range
to teach me how to shoot. She told me to keep the ear
protection on at all times, but I had taken them off once
because—"

"Connie," Trace said, pulling her from her ramblings.

"Sorry. I guess I'm just… Anyway, one of them shot
him. People were whimpering and crying, and I just lay
there. I was praying that I wouldn't be next and I—I
didn't do anything to stop them or to help Richard."

"There was nothing you could've done for Richard,
especially at that point. If you had tried, you could've
gotten yourself killed and possibly everyone else, too.
You did the right thing staying put. That way, you could
tell the authorities everything you saw and heard."

Connie knew he was right, but that didn't stop the
guilt from eating at her. Maybe she could've distracted
them. Maybe she could've screamed or acted out so that
they would've left Richard alone. She just wished she
could've, or would've, done *something*.

"They didn't have to shoot him. They could've just
roughed him up. Not that that would've been any better, but at least he wouldn't be fighting for his life. At

least his family wouldn't be worrying about whether he's going to live or die."

Trace nodded, still studying her. Connie wasn't sure what was going on in his head, but the intensity of his stare was a little unnerving.

She swallowed and glanced away. "I heard the robbers run by me. I thought they were gone, but one had stopped near the exit." The tightness in her chest squeezed with each word as the scene replayed in her mind. "He started lifting the black mask up from his neck. That's when I saw part of his tattoo."

"What type of tattoo?"

Connie shrugged. "Just an elaborate-looking tattoo. It didn't look like the tribal one you have," she said, heat rushing to her face.

She had seen his impressive body art on the night they'd spent together. It was located on the right side of his chest and torso, and a portion of it wrapped around his shoulder and upper bicep. No one would ever know he had a tattoo unless he went shirtless.

"I might be able to get my hands on a copy of the sketch," Trace said, more to himself than to her. He pulled his cell phone from his front pants pocket and typed something.

Connie wasn't sure how he planned to get a copy, but she had learned early on that Trace was resourceful, and she knew he had connections.

"Tell me what else you remember," Trace said, giving her his full attention again.

"I only saw a small portion of the tat. I'm not even sure the description I gave the cops will help." Connie stopped and took a breath. Then her mind took her back to the moment when she and the robber made eye contact. "He stopped."

"Who stopped? The robber?"

She nodded. "He stopped lifting the mask. Turned. Then his gaze met mine. His eyes were an unusual gray. Almost silverish." Connie debated whether or not to tell him this next part, something that had been nagging her since leaving the bank. "There's a part I didn't tell the cops. Mainly because I didn't want them to think that I was in any way part of the heist, but the man's eyes seemed…familiar. Like maybe I'd seen them before. I know it sounds crazy, especially since I don't know anyone with gray eyes, but it was a *feeling*."

Trace huffed out a loud breath and ran his hand over his mouth and down his chin. "Damn," he mumbled and sat back in his seat. "And he saw you."

"It was only a second, if that long. Like I said, everything happened so, *so* fast, and I'm sure I've never seen him before."

"But, sweetheart, he *saw you*. I don't care if it was one second or two. It was a second too long. For all we know, the guy has a photographic memory. Or, like you, he might've thought you looked familiar, too."

"Are you trying to scare me? Is that what this line of questioning or conversation is about? Because if it is, it's not working. I'm not afraid," she said with the conviction of someone wanting to believe her own words. "The FBI agents said that my name would not be released for any reason. Everyone in the bank was questioned. We're all witnesses, and I didn't see much of the one robber. I probably couldn't even pick him out of a lineup if I had to. I'm not afraid."

"I'm glad you're not, but I am. I don't like any of this."

Trace started the car and glanced around the lot as if looking for something or someone. Connie could easily see out, but his car windows were tinted so dark, there was no way anyone could see into the vehicle. She wasn't sure why that thought set her at ease—a little—but it did.

In her heart, she was sure the robber wouldn't recognize her even if he passed her on the street. Yet a small part of her kept wondering…what if he did?

# Chapter 4

"Are you sure you're okay? You're always trying to be strong and act like nothin' is wrong. You did it when Quincy's trifling ass stole your job, and you're prob—"

"Erica, don't go there," Connie said in a warning tone. She gripped her cell phone tighter, needing her sister not to bring up that situation. Hearing her ex's name brought back one of the darkest times in Connie's life. She could admit to picking the wrong men more times than not, but *that* time had cost her much more than a broken heart.

"What I'm saying," Erica continued, "is that me and Nakia wouldn't mind coming over and keeping you company."

Connie's hand shook as she poured herself a small glass of wine. She'd been home for hours, and her frayed nerves seemed to be getting worse the later in the day it got.

After leaving the police station, Trace had dropped her off at the office. She thought for sure she'd be able to get some work done before the end of the day. That didn't happen. Between gazing off into space every few minutes and Trinity hovering over her, Connie had given up.

Like Trace, Trinity had insisted on knowing every detail of the bank incident. She had even suggested assigning her personal security. Connie shot down that idea with the quickness of a striking rattlesnake and then drove herself home.

Now she was tempted to take her sister up on her offer, but didn't want to impose. "Thanks, sis, but I'll be all right. Besides, Nakia has school tomorrow. You'd have to get up crazy early in the morning to beat traffic and get her there on time. I'm going to finish cooking, veg out in front of the TV until I can't keep my eyes open and then go to bed."

After a long silence, her sister said, "Okay, but if you change your mind, we'll come over. Or you can always come over here. Actually, that's a good idea. I'm sure Trinity wouldn't mind if you worked remotely or if you went into the office a little later."

"I know she wouldn't mind, but I do. Listen, I'm going to go about my life the same as usual. That'll help me move on from this incident. Oh, and remember, you can't tell anyone that I witnessed anything at the bank. The fewer people who know, the better."

She wasn't too concerned that her parents would find

out. Actually, even if they knew, Connie wasn't sure she'd hear from them. Their mother lived in Florida with her new husband and barely stayed in touch, while their father, who had walked out when Connie was ten and started another family, lived in Germany.

"I just want to forget all about today."

Connie already knew it would be a long time before she forgot, though. Especially since there were moments now when she could still hear the popping of gunshots and the panicked screams.

"My lips are sealed as long as you call me every day. Heck, more than every day. Call me a few times a day to let me know that you're all right."

"What's wrong with Auntie?" Connie heard her niece ask about her in the background. True to her word, Erica only told her that Connie had had a bad day and was feeling a little down.

"I'm sure she'll appreciate that, sweetie," Erica said, her voice muffled before she returned to the conversation with Connie. "Your niece said she hopes you feel better. She said if you want, you can call her and she'll tell you some new knock-knock jokes."

Connie laughed. "I just love that kid. I might take her up on that offer."

"I'll make sure I tell her. As for you, try to get some rest, and remember, I'm only a phone call or thirty-minute drive away."

"I know, sis. Thanks."

"Oh, and don't forget," Erica hurried to say. "I want you to look at a couple of houses with me after work tomorrow. I'll even treat you to dinner afterward."

"Sounds good to me."

After the call ended, Connie set her cell phone on the counter and glanced at the ingredients for a rigatoni dish. "I'm not really feeling pasta," she mumbled. Instead, she pulled out bread, eggs and milk for her famous cinnamon French toast. Breakfast for dinner always made her feel good, she thought as she hunted through the cupboard for spices.

Thirty minutes later, she inhaled deeply, relishing the comforting scent of hot maple syrup that would go along with her small feast. The tall stack of French toast with a side of sausage and hash browns brought a smile to her face as she loaded up the breakfast tray. There was no way she could consume it all, but Connie planned to eat until she couldn't eat any more.

She set the tray on the living-room table and returned to the kitchen for another plate, syrup and something to drink. Before she could head back, her cell phone rang. Scooping it up from the counter, Connie glanced at the screen and couldn't hold back the smile that broke free.

*Trace.*

"I'm a wuss," Connie muttered to herself.

She had vowed not to call him, even though he'd told her she could. And now he was calling *her*. She was also determined not to fall for his charm, but who was she kidding? She was crazy about the guy.

*We are just friends. Nothing else*, she reminded herself.

"Hello?" Connie finally answered, but the call had dropped. She hit Redial.

"Screening your calls?" Trace's deep voice boomed

through the phone, sending a delicious tingle to the soles of her feet.

"Nope, I wasn't. I didn't get to the phone in time. What can I do for you, Mr. Halstead?"

"Just calling to see how you're doing."

"I'm—I'm all right. I have moments when my mind takes me back to the bank. I'm sure that'll probably be the case for a couple of days, but I'll be fine." Seemed like she'd said that a thousand times in the last ten hours.

"What are you doing?"

Connie strolled back into the living room and sat on the sofa. "I'm getting ready to have dinner."

"What are you having?"

She wanted to say that she was having blackened salmon or a T-bone steak or something equally exciting. Then again, she couldn't wait to dive into what she had prepared. Her stomach even growled in anticipation.

"I'm having breakfast for dinner." She gave him a rundown of her feast, adding a few adjectives to make it sound like a five-star meal.

Trace chuckled. "Melt-in-your-mouth French toast? Seriously? I'm gonna need to try that. Want some company?" he asked at the same time the doorbell rang.

Connie bolted out of her seat. "That depends." She glanced down at her lounging pajamas. The pink shorts set was cute, but maybe not exactly the best outfit for male company. Especially a man that she was seriously attracted to.

"Depends on what?" Trace asked, humor in his voice.

Connie made a mad dash down the short hallway to

her bedroom and tried not to breathe hard. No sense in letting on that she was running to do a quick change.

"It depends on whether that's you ringing my doorbell. But I doubt you'd show up without calling first," she teased.

Moving the cell phone back and forth from one ear to the other while she quickly undressed, Connie tried to do it without sounding out of breath. Within seconds, she had stripped out of the shorts and into yoga pants and an oversize T-shirt.

"Well, if I was at your door, would you let me in?"

"Maybe." She glanced in the hallway mirror. Her curly hair was piled on top of her head with a hair clip. A few long tendrils had slipped out and framed her face. She looked carefree, like she wasn't trying hard.

*Perfect.*

"What if I told you that I had a surprise for you?" Trace asked.

Connie headed to the front of the house, grinning so hard her cheeks ached. Considering they were just friends, she shouldn't be filled with so much giddiness and joy. Yet that was exactly how she felt.

"I'd say I love surprises." She looked through the peephole, then opened the door and disconnected the call. "I have to see the surprise before I'll agree to let you in."

Her gaze traveled the length of Trace, whose imposing size—he was over six feet tall and two-hundred-plus pounds—filled the doorway. He had shed his suit and now sported a white T-shirt that stretched across his wide chest and molded over his large biceps and flat abs. Dark blue jeans covered his legs and emphasized his tree-trunk-like thighs.

She had to stop herself from licking her lips. Her gaze made it back to his handsome face, and that cocky grin that she adored was in full force. Clearly, he knew she liked what she saw. Just having him in her presence was a welcome surprise, but then she noticed the plastic container in his right hand.

"Are those what I think they are?" she asked, her mouth watering in anticipation. It was as if she could already taste the dark chocolate melting on her tongue.

"If you think they are my famous *to-die-for* cookies, you would be right."

"Oh, my." His chocolate-chip cookies with oatmeal, coconut and walnuts were *everything*. Connie opened the door wider and moved aside so he could enter. "Please come in."

Trace laughed as he stepped across the threshold. "I figured these would get me inside. I also brought my famous hot chocolate." He held up a metal thermos.

Connie closed the door. "You do realize that it's still eighty degrees outside, right?"

"I do, but I figured you'd have the air conditioner blasting. Besides, my hot chocolate is amazing any time of the year, especially since it contains a special ingredient." Trace strolled farther into the house, as if he owned the place, and headed to the kitchen.

"What's the special ingredient?"

He rinsed his hands in the sink and opened a couple of cabinet doors before he found the one that contained her mugs. "Whiskey."

"Hmm, sounds interesting. There's only one problem with your surprise."

He filled both mugs and glanced up at her. "What's that?"

"There's no way I can have French toast, cookies and hot chocolate. Too much sugar. I'll be bouncing off the walls like a two-year-old."

"I see."

Trace glanced in the living room, where she had set up her dinner. With the partially open floor plan, he had a slight view of the cocktail table in front of the sofa.

"Well, how about I help you eat the French toast and other fixings? Then you can have a cookie and maybe save the not-so-hot chocolate for when you get ready to go to bed. I guarantee it'll help you have a good night's sleep."

Connie wanted to tell him that if he stayed the night and shared her bed, she'd have a great night's sleep. But she kept that thought to herself. No sense in playing with fire.

"That works for me." She followed him out of the kitchen, but remembered he needed something to eat off of. "Let me grab you a plate. Make yourself at home."

Excitement bubbled inside her. Connie had been prepared to spend the evening alone, but she was glad she didn't have to. In addition to getting a plate and utensils, she grabbed a couple of bottles of water.

She pulled up short when she returned to the living room. Trace had just put a forkful of food into his mouth.

"Seriously? You couldn't wait until I returned?"

"I could've, but I was starving. This is really good. The powdered sugar is a nice touch. It also tastes like you added vanilla and maybe…nutmeg?"

"That palate of yours is on point. I added both, along with cinnamon. You're not the only cook in the room, you know. I can do a little something-something in the kitchen, too."

Not only was Trace a great baker with a few secret recipes, but he was also an amazing cook. On several occasions, he had even made her and Trinity a few dishes to try.

While eating, she and Trace chatted and laughed through one of her favorite sitcoms. Doing something as simple as watching TV and eating breakfast for dinner reminded her of how well she and Trace got along. On most days, in his suit and tie and wearing a pair of Stacy Adams shoes, he looked as if he could be the CEO of a *Fortune* 500 company. Serious and in charge. She loved the professional side of him, but this side was her favorite. Down-to-earth, making a pig of himself and relaxing as if they spent every night together.

"So how are you really?" Trace asked when he finished eating. He leaned back and stretched his arm on the back of the sofa. "Be honest."

Connie curled her legs beneath her as she thought about his question.

"Honestly, I'm better now that you're here."

That lopsided grin that she adored tilted the left corner of his tempting lips. It should be against the law for any man to be so good-looking. The way his full lips curled a little too perfectly and the way his eyes twinkled with mischief, even in the dim lighting, made her heart thump a tad bit faster.

Connie lifted her hand when he started to speak. "Before your head explodes with that big ego of yours, let me finish. You're a good distraction. Before you arrived, every few minutes my mind drifted back to what took place at the bank. It seems surreal. Even though the incident went by fast, in my head it plays out in slow motion."

Trace lightly brushed a strand of her hair out of her face. "Did you remember anything else?"

"No. I think I told them everything, except for what I told you about the man's eyes seeming familiar. Right now, though, I'm just praying Richard will pull through."

"Yeah, hopefully he will."

"I can't help wondering how long it will take for me to put the whole incident behind me."

"It'll probably take a while."

"Is that how it was when you left the navy?" He had done two tours in Afghanistan and spent a few years in Japan, but rarely discussed his military days.

The only sound in the room was the television as the silence between them grew. Connie wasn't sure if discussing that time in his life was off-limits. But that only made her more curious about his experience.

"It will take a lifetime to forget what I went through... what I experienced and what I saw. Each day that I'm away from the military gets easier, though. But occasionally, someone will say something or something will happen that will trigger a memory."

"What happens when you're triggered?" she asked, truly curious.

Again, seconds of silence ticked by without Trace responding. He leaned forward and grabbed his water, guzzling half of it before setting it back on the table. Still he said nothing.

"Want to talk about something else?"

"Yeah, that would be good."

"Okay, well, I was planning to find another comedy show or movie to watch. I figured laughing would do me good. You interested?"

His left eyebrow lifted skyward. "You already know I'm interested," he said suggestively.

Connie punched him in the arm. "I'm talking about the show. Nothing else."

Trace chuckled and reached over her, giving her a whiff of his enticing cologne before he grabbed the remote. "In that case, let's see what's on."

He pulled up the channel guide and scrolled through the list.

"I'mma run to the bathroom real quick. Be right back." Connie hurried down the hall, and once she finished, she went to the kitchen. "I'm grabbing a cookie. Do you—?"

A large boom sounded from outside, and Connie jumped. A second later the lights and television went out. She stood frozen in place as panic bubbled inside her. Had the robbers found her? Had they cut her power?

Alarm bells sounded off in her head as dread seeped into her body. The house was pitch-black, and a dense silence as thick and heavy as San Francisco fog filled the space. Disoriented, her heart practically pounding out of her chest, she fumbled around the kitchen until she bumped into the counter.

"T-Trace?"

"I'm right here," he said calmly, but his voice still made her jump, and she gripped the counter tighter.

"I c-can't see you."

Suddenly, the space was illuminated by his cell-phone flashlight. The room was still dimly lit, but at least she could see him. He moved closer and glided the backs of his fingers down her cheek. The tenderness of his touch sent heat coursing through her body like warm honey and almost made her whimper. How could someone so big, strong and powerful also be so sensitive and gentle?

"You all right?" he asked, standing close enough for her to see concern in his eyes.

Connie gave a small laugh as her insides quivered. She wasn't sure if she was feeling anxious because they'd been plunged into darkness. Or if it was because of his closeness. "I've been better," she said.

Trace moved in even closer and lowered his head. His lips brushed over hers in a soothing manner, and Connie immediately felt more at ease. The kiss was like a whisper over her mouth, but just as powerful, as if he'd slipped her some tongue.

"How do you feel now?" he crooned, still standing close enough for them to kiss again.

A smile spread across Connie's face. "Better. Much better."

"Good. Now let's figure out what's going on with the lights."

"Do you think they found me?" Connie asked, but wasn't sure she was ready for the answer.

"If they had, they probably would've revealed themselves by now. Give me your hand." She grabbed hold tight enough to cause pain, but all he said was "Let's look outside."

With the light from his phone guiding their path, Trace carefully pulled her back to the living room and over to the window. The blinds were closed and he lifted one of the slats slightly and peeked out.

"Do you see anyone?" she asked.

"Damn, looks like there's a power outage in the neighborhood. It's darker than a cypress swamp out there."

"You didn't just allude to James Weldon Johnson, did you?" Connie asked in awe, stunned that he was familiar with "The Creation."

Trace chuckled. "Not exactly, but why do you sound surprised? I do read, you know. And I happen to be a fan of Johnson's work."

The tension inside Connie started to ease. "Duly noted. Seems I learn something new about you every day."

"Funny, I thought the same thing about you earlier." Trace held on to her hand as they moved away from the window. "I'm looking forward to learning even more, but right now, we should probably light the candles that are on your mantel."

"Good idea. I have more around the house, but that'll

be a good start. Can you shine your phone back into the kitchen so that I can get the lighter?"

For the next few minutes, Connie lit the candles in the living room, then went to the guest bathroom and lit the one on the vanity. She had two flashlights in the laundry room and brought them to the living room.

Once she was done setting out additional candles, Connie sat on the sofa next to Trace. Her main goal was to add more illumination to the space, but now, as she glanced around, the area appeared more romantic than intended.

"This is cool. All we need now is some music." Within seconds, soft jazz flowed from his cell phone. "I would suggest I open a couple of windows, but it's probably hotter outside than it is in here."

"Crap, I forgot about the air conditioner. This would be a great time to have a generator."

"Yeah, it would. I looked up the power company online, and according to their website, they know about the outage. A transformer blew in the area and they're working on it, but the site doesn't say how long it'll take to fix."

"I hope not long. I don't want the stuff in my refrigerator or freezer to go bad. Nor do I want us to sweat to death."

Trace slouched down on the sofa, then reached for her hand. "In the meantime, we might as well take advantage of this time."

"Trace." Connie pulled out of his hold and jabbed him in the ribs, which felt like hitting a brick wall. "If you're talking about what I *think* you're talking about, I'm not sleeping with you."

"Dang, woman. Violent much?" He rubbed his side while his lips twitched, as he seemed to be trying to keep from laughing. "And get your head out of the gutter. I meant we could spend this time getting to know each other better, and I'm not talking sexually."

Connie laughed. "Oh. What did you have in mind, then?"

# Chapter 5

"When I suggested we play Twenty Questions, I didn't mean that you'd be the only one to ask them," Trace said on a laugh. "The object of the game is for you to ask me a question, then I ask you one. You've asked at least five back-to-back in the last ten minutes without giving me a chance to ask any."

"Oh. Well, you need to jump in." Connie shifted on the sofa, pulling her legs beneath her. "Each time you answered one of mine, you made me think of another one."

Trace couldn't have planned his visit better if he'd tried. Stopping by Connie's place without calling ahead had been risky. Now he was glad he had taken the chance. He couldn't remember when he'd last had such a nice evening. Working several assignments in a row for almost a month had limited his and Connie's interactions, but tonight felt like they were making up for lost time.

More than anything, though, she seemed to be handling the day's events better than he'd expected. Worrying about her being alone had driven him to come up with the plan of making cookies and dropping them off. Especially since he loved feeding her sweet tooth. Aside from the little freak-out moment she'd had when the power went out, she'd acted pretty normal and was handling herself well.

*Do you think they found me?*

Her question had taken him by surprise, but it let him know that the bank robbery wasn't far from her mind. Though it was a reasonable question, it hadn't been his first thought. Trace wasn't sure how long it would take for the electricity to be restored, but he'd stick around for as long as she needed him.

As he watched her now, the flicker of flames from the candles bathed her copper skin in a combination of light and shadows. Connie was one of the most beautiful women he'd ever met, and the fact that she didn't appear to know it made her that much more desirable.

He played with a long strand of her hair that framed her face and twirled it around his finger. He just wanted to touch her. When he'd kissed her earlier, he thought she would've reprimanded him. Instead, the feathery peck he had placed on her lips seemed to calm her some. Which was the response he'd been going for. It was a risky move. Not because he thought she would get mad. No. The risky part was him wanting more from her.

He'd be lying if he said he didn't want a repeat of the night they had shared together.

"What's something that no one knows about you?" Trace asked.

Her brow furrowed as she tapped her finger on her cheek. "Hmm, that's a good question. I can't think of anything off the top of my head."

"Come on. There has to be something. Did you run the New York City marathon in under two hours? Can you hop around on one leg while holding a plate and eating with a fork? Do you have a weird fetish? You gotta give me something, and I'm talking something good."

Laughing, Connie shook her head. "You are too funny. Well, I don't have any fetishes. At least none I'm aware of, and though my balance is pretty good, I'm not sure I can do the whole hopping-and-eating trick. The only thing I can think of that most people don't know about me is that I sleep with a Cabbage Patch doll."

Trace stared at her, trying to determine if she was serious, and then threw back his head and burst out laughing. He almost didn't recognize the sound. His stomach tightened, and he couldn't remember the last time he'd hooted and hollered the way he was doing right now. Pounding on the sofa, he tried to stop and catch his breath, but when he glanced at her frowning at him, his laughter started all over again.

Connie punched him in the arm. "Would you knock it off? It is *not* that funny."

"I—I'm sorry, but come on. You know that's funny," he said, holding his stomach and struggling to pull himself together. He wiped the corners of his eyes with the back of his hand.

"I'll admit it's a little funny, but dang, Trace." She chuckled. "You're acting like you just sat through a Dave Chappelle skit. I pour my heart out to you and this is how you respond?" she said dramatically, but now began laughing herself.

"Okay. Okay, baby. I'm sorry." He squeezed her hand and leaned back against the sofa, still panting. "You just caught me off guard. So, does this thing—I mean, your doll—have a name?"

"*His* name is Vinnie Montell," she said proudly.

Trace lost it. He laughed so hard, he fell onto his side and rolled right off the sofa. That made him laugh even harder. Still howling, he stumbled to his feet, barely able to catch his breath.

"Ugh! I can't believe I told you."

He dodged the sofa pillow Connie threw across the room at him and was glad it didn't hit one of the candles.

"If you tell anyone what I just told you, so help me. I will…I will…I will never speak to you again, and I'm serious!"

When Trace finally pulled himself together, he dropped back onto the sofa, totally winded. "I promise. I won't tell a soul. Besides, no one would believe me, anyway."

"Oh, shut up."

After several long minutes, when he could finally talk again without laughing, he asked, "What made you buy a doll to sleep with?"

"I didn't. Trinity bought it as a joke one year for

my birthday, and I thought he was cute. I kept him. A few years ago, I was going through a rough patch and wasn't sleeping." She shrugged. "I slept with Vinnie one night and had the best sleep I'd had in months. So I kept sleeping with him."

"Well, if you ever want to replace Vinnie with a real man, I'm your guy."

Connie rolled her eyes, trying to look annoyed, but Trace didn't miss that she was fighting hard not to smile.

He wasn't sure what else to say. If another woman had told him she slept with a doll, he'd probably find an excuse to leave, but this was Connie. She was one of the most put-together people he'd ever met. This info about her was a bit strange, but who was he to judge? His sister and brothers called him strange for one reason or another. He had to admit, though, sleeping with a doll as an adult was…different. Trace was just glad she hadn't needed it the night he had stayed over. Now, *that* would've been weird. If she took a chance on him, she'd never need Vinnie Montell as a sleep mate again.

"Okay, enough about me. What about you? Same question. What's something that no one knows about you?"

"Well, I can't think of anything as…intriguing as your confession, but most people don't know that I play three instruments."

"What?" Connie leaned away and stared at him, her mouth hanging open. "How'd I not know that? What instruments?"

"Piano, guitar, and I dabble a little with the saxophone."

"Get out! I *love* a man who can play the sax."

"Good to know. I'll start carrying it with me so that I can serenade you every chance I get."

"I look forward to it. That explains why you usually have jazz playing on the radio whenever I ride with you... But wait. I told you something superembarrassing about myself, and that's all you've got?"

Trace shrugged, trying not to fall out laughing again. "What can I say? I don't have any unusual details to share. I guess I'm just perfect."

Connie tsked and waved him off.

For the next few minutes, they lobbed questions back and forth. Her responses gave Trace more insight into who she was, but didn't go as deep as he would have liked. There was so much he wanted to know, but he was careful in what he asked, not wanting her to shut down on him.

"If you could trade lives with someone, who would you choose?" Connie asked.

Trace played with a strand of her hair that had fallen out of the hair clip, twirling it around his fingers as he thought about the question. His mind took him back to a time in his life that he'd tried to bury for the last twenty-plus years. "In high school, my senior year, there was a time when I wanted to be *any*body but myself. My self-confidence took a big hit after I let someone's degrading words get into my head. It took me years to rebound from the damage this person caused."

He would never forget that time in his life. Edward Sanderson, a man he once looked up to, treated him like he was the lowest form of human life. Like he was a nobody. All without really knowing him. What Trace wouldn't give to show Sanderson the man he had become.

Connie placed her hand on top of his. "That sounds awful. Who was the *somebody*?"

*Damn.* He should've known there'd be a follow-up question. "Let's just say it involved senior prom, a girl and her father. I'll save the rest of that story for another day. Believe it or not, I haven't always been as confident, good-looking and irresistible as I am now."

"Oh, please. Arrogant much?"

Trace chuckled. He knew that response would distract her. "Hey, what can I say? I'm an amazing guy."

"Yeah, whatever."

"It's true, but, anyway, it's my turn to ask a question. Why won't you let me take you out on a real date?" There, he'd asked it. The question had been burning a hole in his mind since that night they spent together. She had given him a half-assed excuse when he'd asked back then. This time, he was hoping for more detail.

Connie pulled on the collar of her T-shirt and moved her head back and forth. "Is it getting hot in here, or is it just me?"

"Yeah, it's hot. If you want to strip out of your clothes, I wouldn't stop you." She narrowed her eyes at him. "What? I'm serious. That's a good way for you to cool off."

"You are not getting me out of my clothes, Trace Halstead."

"Then maybe I should take off mine." It was definitely getting warm in the house since the electricity was out and the air conditioner wasn't working.

"Don't you dare."

He gave an exaggerated sigh. "Fine. I guess we'll sweat it out. Answer the question while I open a couple of windows." It should've cooled off some outside, or at least he hoped.

"I already told you why I can't go out with you. I have a rule—I don't date coworkers."

"That's what you said, but I have a feeling there's more to that rule."

"'Let's just say…'" she mocked him and smiled, but then turned serious. "It's not just about the rule, but that's a big part of my reason. Trace, I have, um, trust issues when it comes to men. I also haven't made the best dating choices, which is why I'm taking a break and focusing on my career right now."

Trace opened the last of the three windows and wondered when the electricity would be back on.

"I would never hurt you, Connie. I'm making it my personal mission to prove to you that I'm trustworthy," he said when he returned to the sofa.

Connie didn't say anything. She lifted her mug of hot chocolate and took a few sips.

Trace placed his hand on her back. He couldn't help himself. His hand moved in small circles along her spine, and he was glad she didn't pull away. Being here with her felt natural, like hanging out in the evenings together was their norm. He wanted to continue getting to know her because what he knew so far, he liked.

"I'm planning to help you forget every man who

came before me. It's time you learned we're not all chumps."

A smile played on Connie's lips before she gave a little laugh. "I didn't say they were chumps. At least not all of them. Okay, maybe most of them were, but not all of them."

Trace wanted to be the one to keep her laughing. He didn't know what it was going to take to earn her trust, but he was up for the challenge.

Connie held up her mug. "This hot chocolate is really good. I can taste more of the alcohol now that it has sat for a while."

She set the mug back on the table, and it didn't go unnoticed to Trace that she didn't comment on his intentions. That was okay. She would soon learn that he was tenacious when he went after what he wanted, and what he wanted most was her.

Connie's cell phone rang and she jumped, then placed her hand on her chest. "I think my nerves are shot."

"Yeah, I'd imagine they would be after the day you've had," Trace said as she hurried to the dining area, where she had left the cell phone on the table.

"Hello," Connie said in a rush. "Yes, this is she."

Trace could only hear her side of the conversation, but whoever it was seemed to be doing most of the talking.

Connie gasped. "Oh, no."

Trace stood and slowly moved toward her. His body tensed with dread when her trembling hand hovered in front of her mouth.

"I'm so sorry to hear that, but thank you for telling me. Who can I contact if I want to do something for his family?" she asked in a shaky voice and nodded as if the person on the other end of the call could see her. "Yes, tomorrow would be fine. Thank you."

"What happened?" Trace asked and put his arm around her when she disconnected the call.

"Richard…he didn't make it. He died about an hour ago."

"Aww, man, I'm sorry. That's awful."

Connie pinched the bridge of her nose, and Trace watched her carefully. She leaned on the back of a chair and sighed.

"I can't believe it. I wanted him to pull through. When I woke up this morning, I definitely didn't see my day turning out like this. I keep asking myself how people can be so callous and take a life like it's nothing. It just doesn't make sense!" she snapped.

"I know." Trace started rubbing her back again, wanting to offer some type of comfort. "As long as we live, there'll be people in the world who do senseless crap. But I hope you're not still blaming yourself for not being able to help him."

She shook her head and blew out a rough breath. "I know there was nothing I could do, but it still bothers me that I cowered and did nothing."

Trace grabbed her shoulders and turned her to look at him. "Sweetheart, you probably did more than anyone else did or could've done. You gave the authorities a lead. A lead that they hadn't gotten with the other robberies. With your information and what they should be able to pull from security footage, hopefully they'll have those assholes in custody in no time."

"I hope you're right."

Trace hoped so, too, because the sooner those guys were behind bars, the less he'd worry about Connie. Until then, she was going to see a lot more of him, whether she liked it or not.

# Chapter 6

"I made the right decision in not letting Trace stay the night," Connie said as she drove her sister to the next house that the real-estate agent wanted Erica to see. "Besides, I didn't trust myself."

After hearing the news about Richard's death, it would've been easy to fall into bed with Trace. Anything to take her mind off the day, but she hadn't. She couldn't use him like that, even though she wanted him more than she had ever wanted another man. But since she told him that they could only be friends, she had to stick by that decision and not send mixed signals. It was going to be hard, but she had to stand firm.

"Come on, sis. I hope you're not letting a couple of bad relationships keep you from hooking up with a good guy. I don't know Trace, but from the way you talk about him, I know he's a catch. I can't wait to meet him."

Connie glanced at her sister, then returned her attention to the road. "Who said you're going to meet him? He and I are just friends. Nothing else."

Maybe if she kept telling herself that, it would sink in. Before the electricity had come back on, Connie had struggled to keep her hands to herself. There was no way Trace could've stayed. She would've wanted a repeat of the night they'd shared a month ago.

"I don't agree with you, but, hey, if you want to live the rest of your life alone, then who am I to stand in your way?"

"Sarcasm doesn't look good on you," Connie said as she entered a neighborhood that had a mixture of older homes and new buildings. For the past month, she'd been tagging along with her sister to look at real estate and enjoying every minute of it.

"Thanks for driving today. It feels good to not have to be the chauffeur for a change. Between gymnastics, Girl Scouts and playdates, your niece has me running all over town," Erica said.

"No problem." Connie parked her BMW in front of the house that had a large For Sale sign in the yard. "Besides, your driving makes me nervous. Chauffeuring you around for a change helps me keep my sanity."

"You are not funny." Erica laughed, despite her words, then slowly sobered as she stared out the passenger window at the beautiful home. "I still can't believe I'm actually looking at houses to buy."

The melancholy lacing her words pierced Connie

in the chest. Two years ago, she thought Erica would never recover from the death of her husband. Connie had never seen two people more in love than Erica and Kevin. They had given her hope that a happily-ever-after was possible.

That all ended when Kevin was killed on his way to work. He had stopped to get gasoline and a cup of coffee, but while he was inside the gas station, a robbery was taking place. He and one other person were killed. Erica had been inconsolable, especially knowing she'd have to raise their daughter alone. Nakia had been five at the time.

Connie had been living in Los Angeles, overseeing LEPA's other office. She had spent a few weeks with her sister and niece after Kevin's death, then made the trip from LA to Vegas once or twice a month to check on them. When Trinity had suggested Connie relocate and run the Vegas office, she'd leaped at the opportunity. It had only taken a couple of months to get her life in order and find an executive to oversee the LA location.

"What do you think so far?" Connie asked as she took in the two-car attached garage that seemed to dominate the front of the home.

Living in Vegas, she was getting used to the desert scenery, and this home's front yard was beautiful. The grassless landscaping, with gravel and mulch, had two short palm trees, cacti, agave plants and a few other blooming flowers.

"Not bad, even though I'm not a fan of the front-facing garage. It's like the first thing I noticed when we pulled up to the house," Erica said.

"True, but at least it's attached to the house, unlike mine." Not only was her garage a stand-alone, but it also could barely accommodate one small car and offered no space for storage.

As they trekked up the walkway, the front door opened. "Hey, you two." Angela, the real-estate agent, stood on the concrete stoop. "Hopefully, you didn't have any trouble finding the place."

Connie followed them into the house. "No trouble at all."

The smell of fresh paint greeted them at the door. The home had a partially open floor plan. The stairs to the second floor were just beyond the living room and a short hallway led to what looked like the kitchen and dining area.

Angela handed them each a sheet of paper. "Here is the home's spec. As you can see, Erica, it's under your budget and still in your daughter's school district."

"That's great."

Looking at the house with her sister made Connie think about her own desires to get married, have a family and move into her forever home. It also had her thinking about Richard. Only minutes before he was shot, she had promised to see him when she was ready to finance another house. Now he was gone. That fact reminded her of how no one was promised tomorrow.

"What do you think so far, sis?" Erica asked.

Connie gave a half-hearted shrug. "Well, considering we're still standing in the foyer, I haven't formed an opinion yet."

Erica side-eyed her and shook her head. "Always a smart-ass."

Angela chuckled and proceeded to show them around.

Connie followed them past the formal living room and down the hall, taking in the travertine floors along the way. As they strolled through the main level, she skimmed the home's fact sheet. The three-bedroom, two-and-a-half-bathroom home was fifteen hundred square feet and thirteen years old.

"The kitchen is outdated, and I don't like how small this island is," Erica said, scanning the tight space with a critical eye. Like Connie, Erica enjoyed cooking. A large kitchen with updated appliances was a must.

"Since this is well under your budget," the real-estate agent said, "you'll still have money left over to make changes to the kitchen and other parts of the house."

"That's true, but I really wanted to just move in and not have to deal with renovations," Erica said. She stood in front of the sliding patio door before the agent opened it.

They roamed through the rest of the home, which was a nice size and had large bedrooms—a good selling feature. Had it not been for the mostly concrete back-yard and the old appliances, Erica probably would've put in an offer. Instead, she told Angela that she'd have to think about it, but wanted to see a few more places.

Two houses later, Connie was ready to call it quits and get some dinner. Once they were back in the car, Erica stared out the window at the last home.

"I really liked that one, but I want Nakia to have a yard with grass."

"Well, if you like it that much, you can have the backyard redone. Get rid of the gravel and add grass, especially if that's the only thing giving you pause."

Connie gave the house one last look before pulling away from the curb. She and Erica discussed their likes and dislikes of all three homes. The last one had checked off most of the must-haves on Erica's list.

"We've seen some nice options this past month," Connie said, dividing her attention between her sister and the road. "Do you think part of your hesitation to choose one is because you're not ready to buy?"

Erica dropped her head against the headrest and stared straight ahead. "I thought about that, and I'm not sure. Maybe. I know it's time to move on and focus on building a life for me and Nakia, but…"

"But you miss Kevin."

"I do. I still think about him every day, but thinking of him doesn't hurt as much as it used to. I think my hesitation is more about the fact that buying a house is a big financial commitment. This time I'm doing it by myself, and it's scary."

"Tell me about it. I had wanted to buy a house for years, but the LA housing market was out of my price range no matter how much money I made. So making the move here, I couldn't wait to purchase my first home. It wasn't until the closing, when I had to sign my name fifty million times, that I started getting nervous."

"Oh, God. I forgot about that part." Erica shook her head. "It was like signing your life away."

"I know, right? But if you know you can afford it, and you believe that you're ready to make the leap, I say go for it. Life is too short to be second-guessing every-thing because of fear."

Connie might've been saying the words to her sis-ter, but she knew she needed to take her own advice. She was famous for overthinking everything, and there had been too many times she let fear dictate her actions, like with Trace. Sure, she was hesitant to get involved with someone at the company, because if the relation-ship went south, working together would be awkward. But regarding Trace, it was more than that. She was ac-tually afraid of opening her heart to another man and then getting hurt. Ultimately, fear was the main reason she was insisting that they just be friends.

"You haven't said much about the bank robbery. How are you doing?"

"I'm okay. I didn't sleep much last night, but hope-fully I'll do better tonight."

"You would've slept great if you had let a cer-tain cutie-pie bodyguard spend the night. Maybe you would've even had a repeat of the infamous one-night stand."

"Oh, good grief. Give it a rest. I shouldn't have told you about that night, and how do you know he's cute? I never told you what he looked like."

"Just a feeling I have and the dreamy expression you wear whenever you talk about him. You try and play down your attraction, but you're not fooling anyone but yourself. You like Trace. *Really* like him."

Those tingles Connie usually experienced when his name was mentioned were back. There was no way she was telling her sister about how nightly fantasies of him had been interrupting her sleep lately. The previous evening had been the only time in weeks that he hadn't starred in her dreams.

Instead, gunshots and screams like she'd heard at the bank had given her nightmares. After waking in a cold sweat at five o'clock that morning, Connie had given up on rest.

"I know your issues when it comes to trusting men, but maybe give Trace a chance. You said yourself that he's like no other man you've known."

He wasn't. She'd had her share of short-term relationships, ending them for one reason or another. It wasn't until recently, when Trinity had called her out on her love-'em-and-leave-'em behavior, that Connie had taken stock of her dating life.

She headed to the Water Street District, where they planned to have dinner. "How'd you do it?" she asked her sister.

"How'd I do what?"

"How'd you learn to trust Kevin?"

She and Erica had grown up with a father who cheated and a mother who was good at pushing everyone away. Unlike what Erica had built with Kevin, the household she and Connie grew up in wasn't a happy one. Their father left when she was ten, and her mother hooked up with one man after another.

As an adult, Connie struggled to make meaningful connections, especially with men. Then a betrayal like nothing she had ever experienced before had rocked her to the core. Unlucky in love, she was tired of trying to weed through the BS, which was why she was taking a break from dating.

"It didn't take me long to trust Kevin. Probably because he never gave me a reason to not trust him. You can't assume that every relationship will turn out like Mom and Dad's. Not that I'm excusing either of them and how they behaved, but they were *so* young when they married."

"That's no excuse to cheat on her," Connie said.

"I know, I'm not saying that it is, but it's one reason their marriage was so rocky from the start. Then it didn't help that they started having kids right away."

"Is that why you and Kevin waited so long before having Nakia?"

"No. We wanted time to enjoy each other. Looking back and considering how things turned out, I wish we would've had more sooner. I never wanted Nakia to grow up an only child."

"It's not too late. You can still have more children." Erica was two years older and, at thirty-two, still in her prime.

"I know, but I can't see myself marrying again. Kevin was my soul mate. Isn't there some type of saying that you only have one?"

"I've never heard that, and whether it's true or not, I hope you don't rule out finding love again and remarrying."

Erica turned in her seat and Connie could almost feel her sister's glare boring into her. "Excuse me? At least I gave it a try. You won't let a man get close enough to see if marriage is a possibility."

Connie sighed and found a parking space near the restaurant. "I know" was all she could say. She wanted to get married and have a family one day, but first she had to start trusting again.

*Easier said than done.*

A couple of hours later, after dropping Erica at home, Connie headed back to the city. Traffic increased as she neared downtown Las Vegas, which wasn't a surprise since it was Friday night. Like so many others, she should be out taking in a show or maybe having drinks with friends. Instead, she was heading home to her quiet house, hoping to sleep better than she had the night before. What she wasn't looking forward to was being alone with her thoughts.

Needing fresh air, Connie turned off the air conditioner and lowered her window a bit. The sounds of highway traffic with tires thumping over pavement, cars whizzing by and horns blowing was almost soothing. The calm of a peaceful ride seeped into her soul and a smile graced her lips.

*All is well in my world*, she thought. *Alive and healthy.* Connie couldn't ask for much more than that these days. She just needed to act like a person who still had her whole life ahead of her.

"Then why am I going home? I should be out doing something fun."

She was a mile from her house and immediately thought about ice cream. Nothing said "I'm alive and happy" like two scoops of anything that included chocolate.

Twenty minutes later, she exited the ice-cream parlor

feeling like a kid on Christmas morning. Apparently, she hadn't been the only one looking for a sweet treat. There were no available tables inside, and the four cast-iron tables sitting out front were occupied.

She couldn't much blame everyone—it was the perfect balmy night for a sweet treat. At eighty degrees, it was still warm, considering it was after nine, but the light breeze made it comfortable.

Connie dragged her tongue around the two scoops of the day's special—chocolate fudge brownie. The delightful brownie chunks melting on her tongue were worth every single calorie. For the last couple of days, her sweet tooth had gotten the best of her. What made it even worse was that she hadn't worked out for two days.

"Tomorrow. I'll go to the gym tomorrow."

Connie quickly slid her tongue along the side of the waffle cone, catching the melting ice cream. Seemed the faster she licked, the quicker it melted. Eventually, she had cleaned off the sides of the cone and went back to licking the scoops.

Her cell phone rang, and she reached into her back pocket, where she had stored it. When she glanced at the screen, an involuntary smile spread across her lips at the sight of Trace's name. It was the first time that she had heard from him all day.

"Hello," she answered.

"Where are you?" he asked, his deep voice washing over her like a gentle caress despite his blunt question.

"So, what? You can't say hello?"

"I'm sorry. Hi."

"Hi, yourself. Since when do you call and ask where I'm at?"

"The bank robbery was an inside job. One of the tellers was working with the robbers. Do you remember the name of the person who helped you?"

"I have no idea, but what does it matter?"

He huffed out a long breath as if he'd been holding it forever. "Where are you?"

"Getting ready to leave the ice-cream parlor. Why?"

"The one by your house?"

"Yes. *Why?* Are you planning another surprise visit?"

"Connie, this may not be anything we should be concerned about, but I just saw a news report and the authorities are looking for that bank teller. I'm calling because… Heck, I don't know. I guess I'm just worried about your safety. The idea of you being alone while her and the robbers are running free doesn't sit well with me."

Standing on the sidewalk and looking out over the dimly lit parking lot, Connie listened as Trace discussed his concerns. It had been a long time since a man had cared enough to worry about her. Though she appreciated that he cared, she wished he would give it a rest. How could she tell him that without sounding ungrateful? She was never going to be able to put the incident behind her if he kept bringing it up constantly.

"The media has been flashing the teller's face on TV and social media. If you saw a picture, would you remember if she was the one who helped you with your banking that day?"

"Maybe. But, Trace, you need to let this go. I'm trying to move on. Right now, I just want to eat my ice cream and pretend that all is right in the world."

"I'm going to text you her photo," he said, as if she hadn't just made it clear that she was done with the incident.

"Fine, but I'm *not* looking at it until—"

"Look out!" someone yelled suddenly. A second later, Connie was shoved hard in the back with enough force to send her catapulting forward, barely missing a parked car. Her phone and ice-cream cone flew from her hands, and an ear-piercing scream ripped from her throat as she slammed hard into the ground.

"Oh, wow. That car was coming right at her," a man said. "I didn't mean to push her that hard, but—"

"Is she okay?"

"Miss, are you hurt?"

"Don't touch her!"

"I got the jerk's license plate number."

Everyone around her spoke at once as Connie was lying facedown on the ground trying to get her bearings. Her mind racing, and her body throbbing, shock and fear warred within her. She slowly lifted her head and blinked several times until tires came into view. Lots of tires.

*What just happened?*

# Chapter 7

"Connie!" Trace hollered. One minute he was talking to her; the next, screams were piercing his eardrums. Then the phone went dead. His voice ricocheted around the interior of his car like a tennis ball bouncing off a wall. His stomach churned with trepidation as he tore out of her driveway.

He took the next corner on two wheels, then floored the gas pedal and flew down the side street. He tried not to think the worst, but his active imagination conjured up one scenario after another. None of them were good. He had to get to Connie. He just hoped she was okay.

"Come on, come on, *come on*!" Trace leaned on his horn, shouting at a driver who had jumped out in front of him. "Drive or get the hell out of the way!"

As if hearing him, the guy turned left at the corner, and Trace took off up the street.

*She has to be all right.*

The thought ping-ponged inside his mind. He had dropped by Connie's house after seeing the news report regarding the bank robbery. Yes, he'd been concerned about her, but mostly, he just wanted to see her. Now Trace was glad he had shown up at her house. Otherwise, he wouldn't be able to get to her now as quickly.

Ten minutes later, he whipped his car into the semi-lit strip mall's parking lot, ignoring the way his tires screeched. He had to find Connie. The lampposts, strategically placed to illuminate the area, didn't provide much light as Trace slowed and crept toward the ice-cream shop. He noticed a handful of people standing near parked cars across from the store. That was when he saw someone sitting on the ground.

*Connie.*

Trace's chest tightened, and he willed himself to stay calm. Yet his pulse was racing like an Indy 500 driver roaring around the track. She wasn't his, officially, but he immediately felt more possessive of her than he'd ever felt for another woman. The thought of her ever being hurt, or worse, tore him up inside.

Trace couldn't quiet his mind as he pulled up. What the hell had happened here? Had Connie fallen? Had someone hit her? Questions continued bombarding him even after he parked and jumped out of his vehicle.

He jogged the short distance and shoved his way into the inner circle. A woman kneeling next to Connie was shining a cell-phone flashlight on her, and his heart skidded to a stop.

Scratches. Blood. Torn blouse. Connie's lip was busted and her chin scraped. The sight of her bruised and banged up hit Trace like a punch to the gut. He crouched beside her and gently pushed a few strands of her hair away from her face. A fierce protectiveness for her consumed him, and he wanted to strangle whoever had done this to her.

"What happened?"

"Trace?" Connie said, her eyes wide with surprise. "What are you doing here?"

"Are you hurt anywhere else?" Trace's voice sounded calmer than he felt as anxiety hammered inside him. His gaze frantically scanned her before returning to her face.

"I'm all right," she said in a rush, but didn't answer his question.

"We called 911." The woman who'd been tending to Connie a moment ago stood. "They're sending the police and an ambulance."

"I told them I didn't need an ambulance," Connie said, her voice quivering. Planting her hand on the ground between them, she twisted slightly, trying to stand, and Trace helped her up. He didn't miss the way she winced with each move.

He looped his arm around her waist. "Stay still until you're checked out and tell me what the hell happened." His voice rose with each word, and though he was trying to remain calm, he knew he was failing miserably.

"I wasn't paying attention and almost got hit by a car. They saved my life."

"I'm Stephanie," the woman who had called 911 said. "And this is my husband, Larry."

Trace nodded a greeting.

"A guy, or whoever was driving, came out of no-where and was flying through the parking lot." Larry rubbed the back of his neck, looking a bit shook up himself. "I was calling out to her, I mean Connie, but she didn't hear me. I couldn't get her attention, so I lunged in front of the car and shoved her out of the way. I didn't mean to push her that hard."

"I'm glad you did." Connie shifted restlessly.

Trace studied her, noticing the awkward way she held her left hand close to her side.

"She hit the ground pretty hard," Stephanie added. "I'm so glad they were able to get out of the way. That car missed her and Larry by *inches*. Then it smacked the back end of a parked car, and you'd think it would've stopped. Instead, the driver plowed out of the parking lot like his ass was on fire."

"I managed to get the license plate number," another man said. "But the windows were too dark for me to see the driver."

More people started talking at once, and Trace picked up a few details from the conversation. Red. Four-door. Camry or Accord. Loud music. Dent on the right side.

He turned when a squad car and an ambulance pulled into the lot and slowed in front of the ice-cream shop. Two officers stepped out of their vehicle and ambled toward the group.

In the meantime, an EMT asked Connie to sit on the back bumper of the ambulance so she could take her vitals and check her out. Trace stayed close, hating the way Connie was downplaying her injuries. Why was it so hard for her to admit that she was hurt? Between her bruises and how gingerly she was moving, it was clear that she was in pain.

There was something else that bothered him. Trace couldn't help wondering if the incident was intentional or really an accident. It might've been irrational to even think it could be connected to the bank robbery, but that didn't stop his mind from going there. Especially if the teller could identify her. It didn't matter that it was far-fetched or that the robbers would know Connie from any other person. It also didn't matter that it was virtually impossible for them to even know what community she lived in. Yet those thoughts were lodged in his brain.

"Can you tell if her hand or wrist is broken?" Trace asked. Connie was still holding her arm close to her body but had the nerve to glare at him through narrowed eyes.

The EMT had Connie move her hand back and forth, then gently pressed different areas of her palm, asking if this or that hurt. Connie winced a few times and said that it ached, but not too badly.

"It doesn't appear to be broken, but it might be sprained. You should get it x-rayed to be sure."

Connie didn't want to be taken to the hospital, and, not wanting to make a scene, Trace kept his opinion to himself for now. He'd wait until they were alone to try to talk sense into her. He had witnessed her stubborn streak on more than one occasion, and the determined set of her jaw said this was one of those times.

"Ride with me, and I'll make arrangements for your car," he said once the EMT and the cops had finished.

"It's not that far. I can drive."

She started toward her car, but Trace blocked her path. "Connie."

"Trace," she huffed and folded her arms, but winced when they made contact with her stomach. That was yet another area that had gotten scraped when she landed on the ground. "I appreciate your concern, but this all looks worse than it is. I'm not helpless."

"Sweetheart, I never said that you were. I'm just trying to… You know what?" Trace threw up his arms. "Fine. Drive. I'll meet you at your place."

Wound tighter than a helical spring, he left her standing there and hopped into his vehicle. He needed to calm the hell down, but right now, Connie was making him nuts. There were so many things he liked about the woman—everything from her vibrant personality to the way she took charge at work. But he had just been introduced to an extreme side of her. Bullheaded. Strong-willed. She might be petite, but she had just made it clear that she wasn't a pushover.

"Now…how to deal with this uncompromising woman," Trace mumbled. The same woman who owned his heart. He might've respected her independent nature, but he had a problem with her not using common sense. And common sense should've told her to let someone help her.

He followed Connie home, and when they arrived, she pulled into the driveway. Her freestanding garage was about thirty feet past the house. He didn't like that it wasn't attached, that the yard wasn't fenced. It definitely wasn't a safe setup, especially for a single woman arriving home late at night.

Trace parked near the side door of the house, then climbed out of his vehicle. As he stood waiting for Connie to exit the garage, he also noted that she needed more lighting on the property. While her neighborhood might've been quiet and relatively safe, he knew criminals were equal opportunists.

Connie finally shuffled out of the garage, looking wearier than she had only minutes ago. She was carrying her purse and laptop bag on her right shoulder, and a sweater in her hand. It was safe to assume that she hadn't been home since leaving work.

Trace strolled toward her, prepared to lighten her load, when a tan-and-white cat darted across the driveway between them. Connie gasped and jerked back, her bags tumbling to the ground.

"Whoa, babe. It's just a cat," he said and reached for her.

"I know," she groaned, pain lacing her words. She bent forward, cradling her left hand against her chest. "Crap. I moved the wrong way, and…"

Trace cursed under his breath. "You need to quit being so damn stubborn and let me take you to the hospital." He picked the bags up from the ground. "This is ridiculous. Clearly you're in agony."

"Let's just give it a day. I'm sure it'll be better by tomorrow if I don't jostle it too much. If not, then I'll see a doctor."

Trace shook his head. There was no reasoning with

this woman. He placed his hand at the small of her back and followed her to the door. Neither of them spoke as she disarmed the alarm and turned on the kitchen light.

"I'm staying the night," he said, bracing himself for the argument he knew was coming. She could be stubborn all she wanted, but she had just met her match. There was no way he was leaving her alone in this condition. Besides, they still hadn't talked about his reason for showing up at her house in the first place.

"Okay, but...do you mind if we go to your condo instead?" Connie asked. The request shocked the hell out of him.

Trace studied her for a moment until she lowered her head and stared down at the keys in her hand.

"Of course I don't mind. Connie, you have an open invitation, you know that. But I have to ask. Why don't you want to stay here? Did something else happen after I left last night...or this morning?"

He set her laptop bag in one of the kitchen chairs and glanced around the open space. The house was as neat as usual, nothing out of place. For the second time tonight, though, his mind was bombarded with questions. This was a woman who'd been adamant about boundaries. Now she wanted to spend the night at *his* place? Something wasn't right, even though he *did* want her in his home. But not like this.

"Did something happen?" he repeated.

"No, I just don't want to sleep here tonight." She started down the hallway that led to the bedrooms. "Give me twenty minutes to get cleaned up and to pack a bag. Then we can leave."

"Wait," he called out in confusion. He followed behind her, then slowed when she stopped and turned to him.

"Trace, just give me a few minutes, okay?"

The exhaustion in her expression forced him to keep his mouth shut. Instead of questioning her request, he nodded, but he couldn't help wondering what she wasn't telling him.

"I'll never understand women," he mumbled under his breath and went to the living room. Trace didn't bother turning on more lights. Instead, he dropped down on the comfortable sofa and rested his head back. Closing his eyes, he played the last couple of hours around in his mind.

Having had the day off from work, he had lounged around his condo for much of the morning. The afternoon consisted of running errands, doing laundry and tidying up his place. All was going well until he was eating dinner and watching the news. That was when he saw the latest report on the bank robbery.

He hadn't been surprised to find out the robbery was an inside job. His issue now, though, had everything to do with Connie. As long as the crooks were at large, he couldn't relax with her traipsing around the city alone. It didn't help that she thought the criminal that she had made eye contact with seemed familiar, or at least his eyes had.

Trace knew he was being paranoid, but he couldn't shake the gnawing going on inside him. A number of what-ifs continued to torture him whenever he saw or heard anything new about the robbery. Nope. He wouldn't be comfortable with Connie going about her business as usual until the robbers were caught. Since he couldn't shake his unease, he'd have to figure out how to become a fixture in her life until the perps were apprehended. Based on how unyielding she'd been for the last half hour, that wasn't going to be easy.

"I think I'm ready," Connie said, stopping between the living and dining rooms.

She had pulled her hair into a ponytail at her nape and changed into a red T-shirt and skinny jeans, with a pair of navy blue Chucks on her feet. She was already cute, but the casual outfit made her even more adorable.

He didn't know what all she had done while in her bedroom, but she seemed more refreshed. Still, that certain spark that usually shone in her eyes wasn't there.

"Oh, and I hope you don't have Vinnie Montell stuffed in that bag. He's not welcome at my house."

She sputtered a laugh and shook her head. "I'm never going to live that down, am I?"

"Probably not."

"Figures. Just let me grab a bottle of water. Then we can leave. Do you want one?"

Trace strolled into the kitchen. "No, thanks. I'm good." He watched as she struggled to open the bottle before she handed it to him.

"Did you take any pain meds?" he asked, then handed the bottle back once he'd opened it.

Connie leaned her back against the kitchen counter and took a swig. "I must have run out of ibuprofen. Do you have some at your place? Or, if you don't mind, maybe we can stop by the store on the way."

"I have some." He moved closer and braced his hands on the counter on either side of her, locking her in place. Her beautiful hazel eyes met his, but she didn't try to move away. "I'm going to ask you again," Trace said. "Why do you want to go to my place?"

Considering how long it took her to answer his question, Trace thought she wasn't going to respond.

"I didn't sleep well, and now I'm thinking that maybe in a different environment..." Her words trailed off.

When she lowered her gaze, Trace lifted her chin with the pad of his finger, forcing her to meet his eyes. In that moment, he wanted to kiss her tempting lips, but he resisted. Their relationship was already complicated enough, with him wanting more of her than she was willing to give. Not to mention criminals who might be after her. No, he needed to tamp down his desire for her and not make things any more awkward.

"I told you before I left last night that if you needed *anything*, you should call me. Why didn't you? I would've come back."

"Trace, I can't ask you to babysit me," she said, a bite to her tone. "I have taken care of myself since before I was an adult and have lived on my own for years. I don't want to impose on you or anyone else, but after the parking-lot incident, I don't want to be alone. I just hate the idea of inconveniencing you."

"Connie, you claim that we're friends, but you don't act like it." When she started to speak, he placed his finger on her lips to silence her. Her eyebrows dipped into a frown, and Trace almost laughed. Maybe touching her mouth was too much, but he needed to make something clear.

"Real friends come to the rescue when needed, and that's what I want to be for you. A *real* friend." He moved his finger from her mouth. "Besides, if I needed you for any reason, would you have a problem with me calling you?"

"No, of course not."

"Then why do you think I would mind?"

"Because..." She started to turn away, but Trace kept her locked in between his arms. "I don't want it to seem like I'm leading you on. I don't want to send mixed signals."

"You've made your position clear about where you and I stand. I respect that. Am I still interested in more than a friendship with you? *Hell, yeah*, and to be honest, deep down I think you want that, too."

Connie's gaze dropped. She didn't deny or confirm his last comment, and that left him hopeful. He wasn't trying to make her uncomfortable, but he wanted her to know that he wasn't going anywhere. Their attraction to each other was getting harder and harder for him to ignore. He sensed that was the case for her, too.

"I've never forced myself on anyone," he continued, "and I don't plan on starting with you." Instead of kissing her senseless, the way he wanted to, he gave her a quick peck on her forehead. "Now, let's get out of here."

## Chapter 8

Connie took several deep breaths and released them slowly as she and Trace rode the elevator up to the twelfth floor of his building. The soft instrumental jazz flowing through the overhead speakers should've helped soothe the tension that had settled between her shoulder blades. It didn't. This was her first time being at his place.

She fidgeted and nibbled on her thumbnail. To say she was a little nervous about sleeping at Trace's condo was an understatement, but that wasn't what had her on edge. Her distress had everything to do with the events of the last thirty-six hours. Had it not been for his presence on both days, she probably wouldn't have been able to keep it together as well as she had.

*Am I still interested in more than a friendship with*

*you?* Hell, yeah, *and to be honest, deep down I think you want that, too.*

Trace's earlier words filtered into her mind. Their feelings were definitely mutual. Connie just wasn't ready to admit that she wanted him in her life as much as he claimed to want her. Not simply as friends. Deep in her heart, she wanted someone she could count on. Someone she could trust. Someone who loved her unconditionally. And that someone was Trace.

But removing the wall that she had carefully erected around her heart would leave her vulnerable to another betrayal. She couldn't deal with that again. On the other hand, if she *didn't* take a chance on him, he would eventually move on. She would be left wondering what could have been.

Connie had never known Trace to have been in a serious relationship, but that didn't mean he hadn't had any opportunities. Even on the way to his place, someone named Sylvia had called him twice, but Trace had ignored her. Connie wasn't naive enough to think there weren't others who were probably trying to get his attention. Others who weren't afraid to let him into their hearts.

She stole a glance at him as the elevator continued to climb. He hadn't said much on the way to his place, but who could blame him? He didn't know if she would bite his head off if he asked the wrong question. Or snap at him for offering to help her in one way or another. One of her character flaws—pushing people away for self-preservation—had reared its wicked head again.

Despite that, Trace was still sticking around. And she liked that.

"Are you mad at me?" Connie asked just as the elevator dinged and the metal doors slid open.

Trace frowned. "Of course not. Why would you ask that?" He reached for her good hand as they exited. As he guided her down the long hallway, their footsteps were silent on the multicolored carpet.

"I figured you were since you've barely said two words to me since we left my house. I know I'm not the easiest person to deal with. If you've changed your mind about me staying, I'll understand. I can call an Uber and go to my sister's place."

"You're not going anywhere. I'm not letting you out of my sight until the cops find the person who ran into you."

"*Almost* ran into me," Connie corrected him. "They didn't hit me. Thank goodness."

"Either way, you're stuck with me for a while. As a matter of fact, I'm not letting you out of my sight until they catch those assholes. So get used to seeing me around. You can be stubborn if you want to, but I can be just as bullheaded."

She tsked. "I think I liked it better when you weren't speaking to me."

Trace glanced down at her and a slow smile appeared, immediately setting her at ease. "The longer this day goes, the more I'm seeing your other traits."

Connie wasn't sure how to take that, but she hated that he'd seen her unyielding side. Even though she knew he was trying to be helpful after the parking-lot incident, she still wasn't able to tone down her Ms. Independent persona.

"This is me," Trace said when they stopped in front of one of the condo doors. "Welcome to my home."

Connie knew when they'd pulled up to the building, and again when he'd introduced her to the doorman, that the place was high-end. Now that they'd entered the foyer of his condo, she could confirm it. *High-end, indeed.*

She slowed when the space opened up to his living area, noticing tall ceilings and the gray bamboo-wood floors. She loved the hardwood and had gotten an estimate for her own house a few months ago.

The family room was to her right. The space resembled something straight out of *House Beautiful.* The walls were stark white and adorned with African artwork, offsetting a large black leather sectional that screamed "bachelor pad." Floor-to-ceiling windows took up one wall, and in the distance, she knew there were mountains, even though the darkness of night hid them from view. What really distinguished the space was the shiny baby grand piano.

"Trace, this place is gorgeous."

Connie turned and saw a dining area and a cook's kitchen with modern black stainless-steel appliances. An eat-at island with a marble countertop divided the two spaces. The black-and-white color scheme rolled throughout the living space, accented by splashes of purple and gray.

"I'm glad you like it. I'mma put your bag in the guest room. Make yourself at home."

He disappeared to the back of the apartment, and Connie strolled over to the piano. She had always wanted to learn how to play, but never took the time to take lessons. Tempted to press on the keys, she stopped herself. It was late. No need disturbing the neighbors with her amateur abilities. Instead, she strolled over to the windows.

The day had started out pretty good and gone wrong later, but this had been a long night, much like the one before. If Connie didn't know better, she'd think a dark cloud was following her around.

As her gaze settled on the scene below, more of the tension in her body slowly dissipated. She stared out at a stunning rock pool that had a magnificent waterfall, illuminated by soft green lights. The landscape included boulders, palm trees, plants and flowers, emitting a spa-like feel. The relaxing sound of gurgling water that floated up to the window reminded Connie of a babbling brook and was like a healing salve to her raw nerves.

"What a magnificent view," she murmured.

"It is, isn't it?"

Startled, Connie whirled around, her hand flying to her chest. "Goodness. You scared me."

"Sorry." Trace handed her an opened bottle of water and over-the-counter pain medication, then stood next to her and gazed out into the night. "This view is what sold me on the place. I looked at a couple of condos and single-family houses not too far from here. They were nice, but this felt like home the moment I walked through the door. I've been here a few years and can't see myself moving anytime soon."

"I can see why. This would be hard to leave."

Trace showed Connie around, telling her a story about each piece of art in every room. The more Connie saw, the more she fell in love with his place. She had only been there a few minutes and already felt at home...and safe.

Not that she was surprised. There was a protectiveness that Trace embodied that made her feel shielded and cherished. What if they became an official couple—would he continue to be that way? Yes. She knew him well enough to know that this side of him that he was showing her was real, and she liked it. She liked *him*. A lot.

"Your place is exquisite, Trace. I might have to visit more often," she said teasingly, but deep down, she knew she wanted to be wherever he was.

"I'm glad you like the place, and you're always welcome here. You're already on the guest list with the doorman, so use your open invitation."

Connie stared at him. "Seriously?"

"Yep. Only those closest to me make the list. So that means I want you to visit."

Unexpected pleasure surged through her body and tugged at her heartstrings. After the way she'd been insisting they just be friends, Connie found it hard to believe that he had added her to his guest list. It might've been a small gesture to him, but to her it meant more than she could ever express.

She rested her hand on his arm and squeezed. "You... you're amazing," she said, her heart bursting with something akin to love, but she wasn't ready to go there. She wanted to say so much more, but she couldn't quite find the words to express just how much she appreciated him. Besides that, after the days that she'd been having, Connie feared she'd start boo-hooing like a baby at any minute. Instead of getting too emotional, she said, "I'll come, but you have to promise you'll let me use your pool. Then it's a deal."

His sexy grin made an appearance, and he placed a lingering kiss against her left temple. "Just say when. Now, have a seat at the table so I can take a look at your hand and wrist."

He had already grabbed a hand towel and compression bandage from the linen closet. Now he was pulling an ice pack from the freezer. The way her hand and wrist were throbbing, Connie was game for whatever he was planning. The ibuprofen hadn't kicked in yet; maybe the ice would help ease the aching.

Connie watched his every move. She'd been on her own for so long, it was nice having someone take care of her for a change. "I can't thank you enough for everything you've done for me."

"Baby, there's nothing I wouldn't do for you." The deep, sensual tone of his voice sent a delicious tingle scurrying over her skin.

God, this man. How the heck was she going to survive the night and keep things platonic? Part of her wanted them to dive into his bed and she have her way with him. However, the other part of her wanted to use this time to get to know him better.

Trace picked up a small remote control and pointed it at a Bluetooth speaker sitting near the coffee maker on the counter. "A Woman's Worth," one of Connie's favorite songs by Alicia Keys, spilled from the speaker.

Trace pulled out the leather dining chair to her right and sat down. "It's swollen," he said after inspecting her hand. The gentle way he poked and prodded stirred something within Connie. He was probably trying to determine for himself that there were no broken bones. But his touch was evoking a different type of pleasure.

"Does that hurt?" he asked, putting pressure on the heel of her hand.

Connie gritted her teeth to keep from flinching. "A little," she muttered and started pulling her hand away, but Trace held on.

Their gazes met and held, and something so magnetic passed between them. Without taking his eyes from hers, he slowly lifted her hand to his mouth and placed a tender kiss on the inside of her wrist. The gesture was as sweet and intimate as if he had graced her with a kiss on the lips.

Connie's heart beat a little faster. How could one simple kiss suddenly heat her body from the inside out? Something intense had flared inside her. Charming was one thing, but this virile man oozed sex appeal and had her wanting to throw caution right out the window.

"I hate that you got hurt," he said, his voice rough with emotion.

His sultry dark eyes held so much compassion. It was like being swathed in a cashmere blanket, warm and soothing, while still seductive. This sweet, gentle giant was quickly getting under her skin, making it difficult to not fall for him even more. It was hard enough trying to stick to the rules she had set for herself. His touch, the way he looked at her as if she was a precious gift—all of it put a crack in her defenses.

Trace wrapped the ice pack with the towel and placed it on her wrist. "You scared me half to death tonight. Talking to you on the phone one minute, then hearing you scream the next freaked me the hell out. I didn't know what to think, or what I would find when I pulled into that parking lot."

"I'm sorry if I worried you." Connie squeezed his thigh and felt his muscles contract under her touch. "I kinda scared myself there, too." She gave a little laugh but sobered as she thought about how that situation could've turned out differently.

What if no one had been outside? What if that guy, Larry, hadn't reacted so quickly? She could've been killed. Then what? Her life would've been over, and she wouldn't have accomplished half the things she still wanted to experience.

*Life's too short to not live it to the fullest.* The words she had spoken to Erica earlier meant even more now. Connie needed to take heed of them herself and quit letting fear rule her life. She also needed to stop being overly cautious about allowing a man to get close if she ever wanted to have a forever love.

"The small bruise on your cheek is barely noticeable, but how does the scrape on your chin feel?"

"It stings a little, but it's not bad. I put some ointment on it before we left my place. It should be fine in a day or two."

Trace didn't say anything, only nodded. After fifteen

minutes, he lifted the ice pack and set it aside. Connie watched in silence as he began wrapping her hand with the compression bandage. He did it with such precision, it was safe to say he must have done it before.

"Do you want something stronger than water to drink? Maybe tequila?" he asked when he was done. Connie tried wiggling her hand. The bandage was snug, but not tight enough to cut off circulation.

"Tequila is tempting, but I'd better stick with water. Especially since I took pain meds not too long ago."

"That's right." Trace went to the kitchen and pulled a beer out of the refrigerator. "Are you in more pain than you're letting on? Because if you are, it's not too late to head to the hospital."

Connie yawned loudly and quickly covered her mouth. "Oh, sorry, and no. I think the ice and the hand wrap will do the trick."

"Well, since you're yawning, maybe you should try and get some sleep. The sheets on the bed are clean and you know where the towels are located. Just make yourself at home."

Connie nodded. She was tired enough to climb into bed, but she wasn't ready to be alone with her thoughts.

"I looked at the picture you texted me earlier," she said, figuring she had surprised Trace if his raised eyebrows were any indication.

He set his beer on the counter. "Was she your teller?"

"Yes, but I don't see why that matters."

Trace's anxiousness when he called earlier had been palpable through the phone line. Even now, as he tapped his fingertips on the counter, he seemed restless. On edge. Connie couldn't understand why he was still hung up on the robbery. Sure, the what-ifs still plagued her, but that was different. She had actually been there. Of course she'd still be playing it over and over in her mind.

"They don't have a reason to seek me out, Trace. I wasn't near the teller when the robbery took place. As a matter of fact, while I was talking to Richard, I'm sure she was helping other people. Like I said before, everyone at the bank are witnesses. The crooks have no reason to think that I can somehow lead authorities to their doorstep."

"Yeah, but you're the only one who admitted to being able to identify one of the robbers."

"Not really. Just his eyes and a little of his tattoo. I'm sure there are tons of people with gray eyes in Las Vegas."

"True, but you said his eyes were unusual and familiar. What if he's someone you know or someone who knows you? Or maybe you've seen him before, but just can't remember where. I'm willing to bet those guys aren't taking any chances that you recall more than his eye color. Besides that, we still don't know if the incident from earlier is connected. They might actually know where you live."

Anything was possible. The second her gaze had connected with the man's, Connie had experienced déjà vu. But outside of work and hanging out with her sister or Trinity, she didn't socialize much. Especially lately, since work consumed a lot of her time.

"I honestly don't think he's anyone I know. I'd remember those eyes."

"What about his tat?"

"I only saw a little of it."

Trace huffed out a breath and pushed away from the counter. "I'm still hoping that Max can get me a copy of the sketch. Maybe it's a prison or gang tattoo. Actually, if that's the case, the Feds should be able to run it through one of their databases. Have you remembered anything else?"

Connie sighed. "Are you going to ask me that every day?"

Trace studied her, and his eyes softened. "Probably."

"Well, don't. If anything else comes to mind, I'll tell you. Until then, let's pretend I was never at the scene of the robbery."

# Chapter 9

At midnight, Trace was sitting up in bed, his back against the upholstered headboard as he flipped through TV channels. A night owl, he rarely went to bed before one or one thirty. This night was no different, except for the fact that he had company. From his vantage point, he could keep an eye on Connie sitting on the balcony that was right off his bedroom. At first, he had thought about lounging in the family room, but with his overprotective nature, Trace didn't want to be that far from her. This way, he could give her some time alone, while still being nearby if she needed him.

The dimmed bedroom lights cast just enough illumination for Connie to not be in the dark. But not so much that would take away from the serenity of being on the balcony, listening to the calming waterfall below.

It seemed surreal to have her at his place. How many times had he imagined Connie spending time in his space or staying the night? This wasn't exactly what Trace had in mind, but he loved having her here. She wanted him to forget about the robbery and everything attached to it, but that wasn't going to happen. He was unsettled, knowing that Connie might easily still be a target. Those guys wouldn't want anyone, a witness or a teller, left behind if there was a possibility that they could be identified.

Trace had talked with Trinity before heading to Connie's place earlier that day. He'd had questions that someone with a law-enforcement background might be able to answer, like what the chances were that the robbers would try to find Connie. She thought the possibility was very slim, but when pressed, she admitted to being concerned.

Trace's attention went to the balcony door as it eased open, and Connie tiptoed in. His gaze traveled the length of her profile. She wore a cute pajama shorts set that wasn't necessarily sexy, but he knew what was underneath the cotton material, and her well-toned, shapely legs were another story.

"I'm not asleep," he said quietly, not wanting to startle her as she closed the door behind her.

"Oh, good. I mean, I didn't want to wake you. I hadn't planned on staying out there so long, but it was so relaxing."

He smiled at the words on her short-sleeved top— *Kiss me, I'm adorable*. Trace wanted nothing more than to do that. However, he had decided that if anything ever happened between them again, she'd have to be the one to make the first move. He just hoped she wouldn't make him wait too long.

"Like you, the balcony is one of my favorite spots in the house. Oh, and I'll make sure there's coffee ready when you get up. That way you can experience the morning out there with a strong cup of joe."

Connie shook her head. "Trace, you don't have to wait on me hand and foot. You've already done so much. The least I can do is fix a cup of coffee. Actually, if you have eggs, bacon or similar food items, I'll even volunteer to make breakfast for us in the morning."

"I wouldn't say no to that."

Connie glanced at the television. "What are you watching?"

Trace had just switched to Netflix and was planning to watch one of his favorite stand-up comedians. He told Connie, then added, "You're welcome to join me if you're not too sleepy." He patted the spot on the bed next to him. He'd been observing her for much of the night, and her tough-guy act wasn't working on him.

No, she was too compassionate. There was no way the incident wasn't at the forefront of her mind. Not only had she been there, but someone she knew had also been killed. She could pretend all she wanted, but she wasn't fooling anyone, especially not him.

"Okay, maybe for a little while," she conceded and climbed onto the king-size bed.

Trace dimmed the lights even more. Not to the point where they couldn't make out each other's features, but enough to help them both relax.

"I've never heard of this guy before, but he's pretty funny."

"He is. I've seen his show in person a few times. I'll let you know the next time he's in town."

"I'd like that. Speaking of shows, I have two tickets to a Broadway musical that's coming to Vegas in a couple of weeks. Do you want to go with me?"

Trace glanced at her, surprised by the invite. He wasn't big on musicals, but for her, he'd sit through one. As far as he could remember, he didn't have anything planned for that day. Even if he had a prior commitment, he'd cancel.

"I'd love to go with you."

Once the show finished, another one came on. Connie was quiet, only laughing every now and then, and her head now rested on Trace's shoulder. If she fell asleep, he'd just carry her into the other room. There was no sense in tempting fate by having her sleep in his bed all night…no matter how much he wanted her to.

Connie felt a peace she hadn't experienced for a while as she lay against Trace. It was nice knowing that they could hang out in his bed and have the interaction not be sexual. She couldn't remember the last time she'd had such a meaningful relationship with a member of the opposite sex. One where there were no expectations. Instead, there was a friendship. Well… more than that. There was someone who wasn't her sister or Trinity that she could call on when needed.

"Thanks again for being here for me these last couple of days," she said.

Trace had turned the volume down on the television, and the only other sound was the subtle hum of the air conditioner.

"I'm glad I could be here for you."

He leaned forward, forcing Connie to lift her head, adjusted the pillow behind him and scooted down until he was lying on his back. Then he opened his arm to her.

"Come here."

Connie hesitated for only a second, then eased down and rested her head on his broad chest. Her body ached some, and the scrape on her stomach stung a little, but it felt good to be in his arms. He wore a navy blue T-shirt that hugged his muscular body and blue lounging pants. He might as well have been naked, though, because her body was on high alert being so close to him.

*Man, he smells amazing.* His signature scent, a woodsy, citrus fragrance that would forever remind her of him, surrounded her like a gentle breeze on a summer day.

Trace held her close to his side. "Relax, sweetheart. I can feel how tense you are. Nothing is going to happen between us unless you want it to. So try to loosen up."

He went back to watching television while Connie did exactly what he suggested. His tenderness was like a soothing balm to her tattered nerves, working its way deep into her soul, while the steady beat of his heart comforted her in a way she hadn't experienced in like... forever. The tension from moments ago—gone. Even though she was exhausted enough to sleep a week, Connie still couldn't seem to shut down her brain.

"Tell me about your family," she said suddenly.

Trace turned toward her slightly and she lifted up, but he kept her in place with a large hand on her hip.

"Where you going?" he asked.

"Nowhere. I thought maybe I was getting too heavy and you needed to move."

His deep chuckle rattled inside his chest. "Sweetheart, as tiny as you are, no one could ever accuse you of being too heavy."

Connie didn't tell him that her father used to call her Tiny when she was a kid. It was funny that she hadn't thought about that in years. She'd been a daddy's girl until she was around eight, but then everything had changed as her parents' relationship started deteriorating.

It didn't take a psychologist for Connie to know that the broken bond between her and her father had a lot to do with her hesitance to trust and allow herself to depend on men. But the more time she spent with Trace, he was showing her that all men weren't the same in that regard. Some could be trusted and counted on to be there when you needed them.

"What do you want to know about my family?" Trace asked.

"Anything you want to share. Maybe tell me how it was, growing up with so many kids in the house."

"It's only four of us, even though with my sister it felt more like eight. She's three years younger than me and was always getting into something. Which was probably good because she kept my dad on his toes. After my mother died, I remember how lost he seemed. He used to say that Mom was the backbone of the family."

"How did she die?"

"A blood clot in her lungs."

Connie's heart thudded against her chest. "Oh, my God. Trace, I am so sorry. That had to be awful."

"Yeah…but it was a long time ago. I was seven when she died. Old enough to remember her, but not old enough to remember many details. Like how she wore her hair, or what her favorite color was, or what she smelled like. What I do remember is that my dad had to work a lot to keep the household going. My oldest brother pitched in with raising us, but we all had to do our part."

Still cradled in his arm, Connie glanced up at him. She was awed by the man Trace had become, despite losing his mother at such a young age. And the fact that he was sharing something so personal about his life only added to her attraction to him.

"Since you enjoy cooking, was that one of your responsibilities?"

Trace smiled. "Actually, I do remember my mother calling me her sous-chef, even though I didn't know what it meant back then. I always wondered if she knew that she was going to die young. She taught each of us different chores, everything from cooking to laundry. After she died, it was like we each were responsible for taking care of things in those areas. Except for my sister." He chuckled. "She was still young, which is probably why she was a wild child growing up."

Connie yawned, exhaustion seeping in even deeper. "You'll have to share some of her shenanigans one day."

"I will. Hopefully, you'll get to meet all of them in the near future."

"I look forward to it." She had already met one of his brothers, Langston, the FBI agent, who had stopped by the office a few months ago to drop off something for Trace.

"Now, what about you? Tell me about your family."

"Not much to tell. Erica and I are real tight, but we aren't… Well, I'm not that close with my parents."

A heaviness settled in her heart at having to admit that to him, but it was true. Her parents might've raised and provided for her, but them arguing all the time and then ultimately splitting up had created a wedge between them that Connie wasn't sure how to fix.

"They divorced when I was a kid, but the last couple of years they were together weighed heavy on our family. My dad cheated on my mother, and our lives were never the same. When my sister and I were old enough to understand, he claimed he had only stepped out on my mother once. Still, my feelings about him didn't change. He cheated, plain and simple. I never could wrap my brain around that. I'll admit, my mother wasn't the easiest person to get along with, but still. How is it that men cheat and think nothing of it?"

"Not all men step out on their women, Connie. I hope you know that."

In her head, she knew it, but in her heart, she always feared that a man would one day cheat on her. Which was probably why she never let a relationship get that far, except for with Quincy.

"Did someone cheat on you? Is that why you won't give you and I a chance?"

Connie stared at the television without really watching the show. Only Erica and Trinity knew about her dating fiascoes, and Connie wasn't proud of the way she'd handled some situations.

"No one cheated. At least as far as I know, but one did betray me in a way that I still struggle to forgive."

"What did he do to you?"

"He stole my job."

Trace turned fully onto his side. Connie didn't make eye contact, but she could feel the intensity of his stare. "How?"

"I landed a job as an analyst a few years before I joined Trinity at LEPA. Quincy, the guy I was dating at the time, worked for the same company. He actually reported to me."

"I assume this story has something to do with why you don't date coworkers now."

"It has everything to do with that rule. Anyway, he and I were together for almost a year before getting engaged."

*"Engaged?"*

"Yep. Which was probably why his betrayal hurt so much. I was interested in the director's position. I had experience. I had been with the company for five years, and I had a ton of ideas. Ideas that I had planned to implement if I landed the job. My supervisor told me about the position even before it had been posted.

"I shared that information with Quincy. Hell, I shared *everything* with him. My life dreams, work ideas, secrets—you name it, he knew every damn thing about me, including my weaknesses," Connie said from between gritted teeth.

Trace ran his hand up and down her hip as she pulled herself together. She hadn't realized how loud she had gotten, but every time she thought about Quincy, she wanted to scream. Or punch something.

"I was in love for the first time in my life," Connie continued.

The sudden bout of anger simmering in her gut was quickly building up steam. She and Quincy had happened so many years ago, but discussing him was bringing back those bad memories.

"I trusted him. I never knew I was capable of trusting until he came along. I also never knew that I could hate someone as much as I hated him after what he did to me. I vowed 'never again.' Never would I allow myself to be that vulnerable."

"What exactly happened?"

"Once the job was posted, I applied. I never knew Quincy was even interested in the position *or* that he had applied for it. At least not until he got the job."

"Wait. You didn't know he interviewed for the position?"

"Nope. I didn't know anything. It worked out that I was traveling for the company and had been on the road a few weeks. I even had my interview over the telephone. Not once did Quincy mention anything about him or the position, and it wasn't like management shared who all had applied."

"Damn. That had to be awkward once you did find out."

"Let's just say that he's probably still trying to put a new wardrobe together."

Trace chuckled.

Connie could laugh at the situation now, but back then, she had been livid, hurt and devastated. She never knew she could get so angry or could hate someone so much. She and Quincy had been living together at the time, and she was glad the apartment had only been in his name. After destroying all his clothes and a few of his personal items, she packed her stuff and moved out.

"So because of that asshole, you won't give another brother a chance," Trace said. "If I ever run into the guy, I'm kickin' his ass."

Connie smiled at the conviction in his statement. "Don't. It was a long time ago, and he's not worth you ending up in jail."

"Yeah, but it would feel good to do some damage to his face for hurting you."

Connie yawned again and her eyes grew heavy. "And I probably wouldn't stop you."

It warmed her heart, knowing that Trace would come to her rescue and help fight her battles if needed. He was such a sweetheart, and Connie loved having him in her life. What if she allowed him to get closer? Would he continue being the amazing man he was proving to be? Or would he turn into another Quincy—just out to get what he could get from her?

# Chapter 10

As they drove to the sandwich shop near the office the next day, Connie couldn't help but smile. It was Saturday afternoon, and she and Trace had spent the morning continuing to get to know each other. As promised, she prepared a huge breakfast, and they'd played Twenty Questions again.

She had never been good at sharing personal information, but Trace had a way of making her want to tell him everything about her. Despite the ice-cream-shop incident, this was turning out to be one of the best weekends she'd had in a long time, bruises and all.

Trace pulled into the parking lot. "Are you still okay with us getting food to go?"

Heavenly Sandwich Shop's name was fitting. Usually, on Saturdays, the day's special included barbecued meat. Whether ribs, chicken or brisket, it always smelled heavenly when you stepped into the building, as if prepared by angels from above.

"Carryout works for me," she said.

They planned to binge-watch a Mafia show on Netflix, then later hang out by the pool once it cooled off outside. Connie had been surprised when Trace had suggested they go shopping for a swimsuit for her. He'd told her that she might as well test out the pool while she was visiting.

At first, she'd been hesitant to agree to spending time at his pool. Not because she was shy or harbored any issues about her body. No, she was very comfortable in her skin. Her uncertainty had everything to do with Trace. She was already struggling to control the potent desire to repeat the night of passion they'd shared a few months ago. And now, imagining him in swim trunks, her body was already heating up at the prospect of seeing his wide chest, broad shoulders and corded muscles on full display. Him practically naked would test the willpower of even the strongest woman. Then again, a little eye candy never hurt anyone.

She glanced at Trace as he shut off the car, wondering why he wasn't making a move to get out. Instead, he turned to her, propping his right arm on the back of her seat.

"What?" she said. He just sat there and stared at her. His gaze volleyed from her eyes to her mouth and back to her eyes again.

"There's something I've wanted to do from the moment you woke up with bedhead," he said, his tone serious, but Connie burst out laughing.

She'd ended up falling asleep in his bed and had the best sleep she'd had in a long time. Maybe she should've been embarrassed to wake up to him looking at her, messy hair and all. Instead, that moment felt right. It felt natural. During breakfast, he told her that he had planned to carry her to the guest bedroom after she fell asleep but hadn't because he liked having her in his bed. And she loved being there snuggled up next to him and wrapped in his strong embrace.

"If this is you trying to sweet-talk or seduce me," she finally said, "you're off to a horrible start." That got a smile out of him, and her stomach fluttered. Fighting her attraction to him was getting harder by the minute.

Without another word, he placed his hand at the back of her head and pulled her closer. "Don't be mad, but I can't help myself."

Not giving her a chance to respond, Trace covered her mouth with his. This wasn't a sweet and innocent kiss like the one from the other night. No, this was serious. This was a you're-mine-and-I'm-yours type of tongue action going on, and Connie was loving every minute of it.

Her arm went around his neck, pulling him even closer and deepening their contact. Her heart thundered with each lap of his tongue as their moans mingled. Boy, could this man kiss. Trace was reminding her of what she'd been missing. Reminded her how good he made her feel, how good they were together.

Why had she put herself on hiatus from dating, or

set the stupid rule about dating a coworker or subordinate? Trust issues? Yeah, those might've still been a part of her, and Connie couldn't exactly quantify just how much he meant to her, but he was also quickly becoming more than a friend.

Trace slowly eased his mouth from hers, but neither of them released each other as they stared into each other's eyes. Connie wanted to kiss him again, and again, and yet again. Hell, she wanted way more than a kiss, but now was not the time. Not just because they were camped out in his car. No, it also had to do with her coming to grips with whether she was ready for all that he was offering. Once she crossed that line with him again, there would be no turning back.

"I'm not apologizing for that," he said with finality.

"Good, because I'm not sorry, either."

"Cool. Then we're on the same page. Sit tight."

Trace climbed out of the car, and Connie couldn't help but smile as he walked around the front of the vehicle. That kiss, though… Clearly, they'd both wanted that to happen, and she was glad he hadn't waited for her to make the first move.

"Thank you," she said when he opened the passenger door.

Trace flashed that sexy grin when he grasped her hand to help her out of the car. "My pleasure."

Connie didn't think she'd ever get used to the tingles that shot through her body each time he touched her. During breakfast that morning, he had asked that she spend the weekend with him, and she'd agreed. It was hard not to when he constantly showered her with attention and catered to her every need. More than any-thing, though, she was enjoying his company, and it was going to be hard to go back to business as usual come Monday.

Trace held on to her good hand, threaded his fingers with hers as they headed to one of the entrances. Since last night, she'd been doing a good job at icing her hand when it wasn't wrapped. There was still a dull ache whenever she moved it a certain way, which was why it was currently wrapped. But it felt a lot better than it had the night before. She could move her fingers just fine, and the swelling had also gone down.

Connie inhaled deeply the moment they stepped into the restaurant. The savory aromas of herbs, spices and wood smoke greeted her at the door. Some people pre-ferred fancy restaurants with great views, but give her finger-licking barbecue and any type of fries, and she was in heaven.

They stood in the shortest line and glanced up at the menu listed on several large boards that hung on the wall behind the registers. Normally, during the week, she ordered a garden salad and a shrimp po'boy or some other sandwich. Today would be anything barbecued.

"What are you getting?" she asked Trace, who was still perusing the menu.

"I'm thinking about the big-boy brisket sandwich with coleslaw and fries. After following you around the mall for the last few hours, I've worked up an appetite."

She laughed and swatted his arm. "Whatever. You know good and well that you were the one pulling me from store to store."

He gave a half-hearted shrug. "What can I say? I wanted you to have the perfect swimsuit."

She actually found two—a yellow two-piece and a baby blue one-piece with a plunging neckline and cut-outs on the sides. They were sexier than she usually went for, but she loved how she looked in them…and imagined Trace staring at her while she tried them on.

"What are you getting?" he asked.

Before Connie could answer, his cell phone rang. He dug it out of his jeans front pocket and glanced at the screen.

"I need to take this. Can you order for me?"

"Of course, and it'll be my treat," she said, but Trace slipped money into her hands and gave her a quick kiss before he strolled away.

He was proving to be one of those men who liked to take care of a woman. They'd have to talk about that later. The last thing she wanted was for him to think that he had to; she didn't mind covering the tab sometimes.

She watched him maneuver around people who were waiting for their order, and she wasn't the only one checking him out. There was a table, near the exit, that was occupied by four women, and all were watching Trace with interest.

Connie wanted to puff out her chest and say *Yeah, he's mine. You can look, but don't even think about touching.*

One of them, the one with a short bob and too much blue eye shadow, glanced at her. The woman smiled, lifted her coffee mug and nodded in acknowledgment. A grin tugged up the corners of Connie's lips. Yep, she wasn't the only one who appreciated the view that Trace provided. Masculine beauty at its best.

The line moved, and before long, Connie placed their order. She couldn't wait to eat. Knowing that the food would be good added to the anticipation.

She stepped to the pick-up counter. While she waited, she pulled out her phone to check her social-media accounts, realizing she hadn't done that since leaving work on Friday. That was unlike her.

"Connie?" the owner's son, Nathan, called. "Connie!" he repeated.

"Right here." She lifted her hand and maneuvered around a woman with two small children.

"Oh, hey, Ms. Shaw," Nathan said. "I didn't know your name was Connie."

"It is, and that's what you can call me instead of Ms. Shaw. How are you? How's your mother?"

"I'm well, and Mom is doing great. She's in back, probably bossing someone around." He gave a little chuckle and handed Connie a large bag of food.

"Thanks, and tell her I said hello."

"Will do."

Connie stepped to the side and grabbed napkins that she stuffed into the bag, plus a few condiment packets. After double-checking that she had everything, she turned to leave, then groaned when her purse knocked over the container of straws, sending every one of them tumbling to the tiled floor.

"Oh, that's just great."

She set the bag of food on the cabinet, then bent down to pick up the wrapped straws.

"Whoops. You missed a few," a deep voice to her right said as he handed her more straws.

"Thank you." Connie stuffed them all into the container and repositioned her purse on her shoulder before standing. "I appreciate your…" The rest of her words stalled in her throat when her gaze collided with the owner of the deep, throaty voice. Familiar gray eyes stared back at her.

*Oh. My. God.*

*Those are the eyes.*

The eyes that had looked so familiar days ago.

"Always nice to help a pretty lady," he said, then narrowed his eyes. "Have we met?"

Connie's pulse climbed higher, and her hands trembled when she set the straw container on the counter. "Uh, n-n-no," she stammered, trying to pull herself together before making a complete fool of herself. She wasn't sure what to say or do.

"You look familiar," Gray Eyes said. "Maybe I've seen you here before."

"Maybe," Connie said, her tone noncommittal. She discreetly glanced at the door that Trace had walked out of, hoping he would hurry back. What the heck was taking him so long? He'd know what to do.

When she turned back to Mr. Gray Eyes, he was gone.

"Oh, no."

Connie frantically looked around as anxiousness clawed through her body. He wasn't in line. He wasn't sitting at any of the tables or standing in the hallway that led to the restrooms. She started down that hall, thinking that maybe he had slipped into the men's room, but another man exited the single-person restroom, confirming that Mr. Gray Eyes hadn't gone that way.

How had he disappeared so fast?

With a tight grip on the bag of food, Connie hurried to the exit that led to the front of the building.

"Excuse me. Sorry. Pardon me," she said as she skirted around people, hoping to get to the guy before he got too far. After pushing open the front door, she glanced left and right, looking past people strolling down the sidewalk. "Where'd he go?" She jogged to the corner and looked both ways.

*Gone.* He was nowhere to be seen.

"Connie?"

She whirled around when she heard Trace's voice. She wasn't sure what he saw on her face, but his brows furrowed.

"What's wrong? What happened?" he said in a rush and took the bag from her and wrapped his other arm around her. "What are you doing out here?"

"Trace, I saw him. The guy. The guy with the eyes."

*"What?"*

Trace pulled her closer and glanced around. "Why would you come out here by yourself? Do you know how dangerous that could've been?"

"I know. I know. I wasn't thinking. I just reacted."

"Are you sure it was him?"

"I—I think so." Connie searched her mind, trying to remember anything else about him. "I'm pretty sure. He had the same eyes. I *remember* those eyes. He also had a scar across his cheek and a five o'clock shadow. Tall, but not as tall as you. Maybe six feet, and lean."

"What about the tattoo on his neck? Did you notice it?"

Connie sucked in a shaky breath, willing herself to calm down and think. She closed her eyes, trying to recall if the guy had a tattoo. When she opened her eyes again, Trace was watching her intently, worry in his eyes.

"I don't know. Dammit. I don't remember seeing a tattoo. Maybe he had one, but I was so shocked to see him, I'm not positive."

"Did it seem like he recognized you? What did he say?"

She told him about the straws and how he had helped her pick them up. "He said it was nice to help a pretty lady. All I could do was stare at him. Then he asked if we'd ever met, and that I looked familiar. I glanced away for a second, and when I turned back, he was gone."

"But you think it was the same guy?"

"I—I think so. Maybe. Oh, no. I'm not sure." She dropped her forehead to Trace's chest and shook her head. "I can't believe this. I'm just not sure. I don't remember seeing a tattoo."

Trace wrapped his arms around her and kissed the side of her head. "It's all right. Let's see if Nancy is here," he said of the restaurant owner. "There are a couple of cameras inside. Maybe she'll let us take a look at the footage."

They headed back down the street toward the restaurant. All Connie could think about was that she might've just let a killer walk away. Why couldn't she have done *something*? At least she could've kept him talking until Trace returned.

Then again, all she'd really noticed at the bank were his eyes. What if this person *wasn't* him? What if he just looked like the robber? The last thing she wanted to do was accuse an innocent man of something he didn't do.

*But what if he really is the man who killed Richard?*

The way her heart was fiercely pounding had her thinking that he was.

An hour later, they entered the condo. Frustration drummed through Trace as he set the bag of food on the counter. Their lunch was definitely cold and he was starving, but he couldn't eat until he got his head on straight. Seeing the mysterious, gray-eyed man again had definitely spooked Connie.

Before they'd left the sandwich shop, Nancy had let them watch the security footage. Unfortunately, it hadn't done much good. There was a shot of the guy picking up straws and helping Connie, but all they could see was his back. The only thing that made Trace think that something was up with the man, aside from Connie's observations, was the way he kept glancing around the restaurant. Like he was up to something and was checking to make sure he wasn't being watched. Unfortunately, he never turned to the camera. Trace wasn't sure if that was intentional or if it was by chance. Nancy mentioned that she had seen him in the restaurant a few times before.

"Considering I work for a security firm, you'd think I'd be more observant," Connie said, sounding dejected as she slid onto one of the bar stools at his kitchen counter. "How is it that I can't remember if this guy had a tattoo? His neck should've been at eye level."

"Babe, you're being too hard on yourself. He caught you off guard. Anyone would've freaked. Besides, maybe you didn't notice a tattoo today because he didn't have one."

"But I'll never forget those eyes. They were the same as the guy at the bank's. I know I sound crazy right now, but, Trace, I'm sure." She slammed her elbows on the counter and gripped the side of her head as if frustrated. "I'm pretty sure."

Trace was at a loss over how to comfort her. She'd basically said the same thing throughout the ride back to his condo. He hated that he hadn't been in the restaurant with her, but if he had been, he was sure the guy wouldn't have approached her.

The telephone call Trace had received while at the sandwich shop was regarding the hit-and-run at the ice-cream parlor. The cops found the driver, a drunk man who had ended up in an accident that wrecked his car, as well as two others. Thankfully, there were only minor injuries to those involved. Knowing the jerk had been inebriated when he'd almost plowed into Connie made Trace doubly thankful that Larry had pushed her out of the way. It was also good to know that the parking-lot incident didn't appear to be connected to the bank robbery. But now that Connie thought she'd seen the robber again, Trace's concern for her safety was at an all-time high.

"Maybe you should stay with me for a few more days," he said and put her food in the microwave.

Connie started shaking her head before speaking. "No. I've inconvenienced you enough. Despite what happened at the restaurant, it's been fun hanging out with you. I'll never forget how you came through for me, but I'm going home tomorrow night."

"Fine. Then I'm going with you." He couldn't stop her from leaving, but that didn't mean he wasn't going to keep an eye on her.

# Chapter 11

Late Monday afternoon, Connie hung up the phone and leaned back in her office chair as she tapped her fingers on the desk. She couldn't for the life of her remember the last time she had seen her wallet. So far, her debit card and two credit cards hadn't been used, thank goodness, and she'd frozen both. If she didn't locate the wallet in the next couple of days, then she would go ahead and cancel them. In the meantime, she was also without a driver's license. "I hate going to the DMV," she mumbled.

Connie first realized she was missing her wallet when she was getting ready for work that morning and changing purses to match her outfit. Thankfully, Trace had insisted on spending the previous night with her and was able to give her a ride to work.

He agreed to look around his condo, but Connie was pretty sure it wasn't there. He hadn't let her pay for anything. The only way her wallet would be there was if it had fallen out of her purse. Now that she thought about it, she'd had it the night she'd gone for ice cream... She absently coiled and uncoiled her injured hand, then wiggled her fingers. Her hand was almost back to normal, but still a little stiff at times, like now.

The events of the last few days felt as if they'd happened a long time ago. Had it not been for her time with Trace, they might've been unbearable. He'd been a fun and wonderful distraction, and Connie struggled to stop thinking about him every few minutes.

Her desk phone beeped twice, letting her know her assistant was calling. "Hey, there," she answered.

"Hey, Connie, your four thirty is here," Jade announced.

Connie glanced at her calendar. Indie Sanderson was her last appointment for the day. She'd already had six consultations with potential clients and had closed the deal with four of them. The other two needed to work out logistics on their end before committing to hiring a security specialist.

"Thanks, Jade. You can walk her back."

Connie stood and glanced down at her outfit. She checked to make sure her floral wrap blouse wasn't showing too much cleavage, and that her tan skirt hadn't twisted on her.

Indie Sanderson was a model who was only in town for a couple of days for a celebrity fashion show, which Connie would also be attending. She was looking forward to the annual event where professionals like Indie, as well as A-list actors and actresses, would be modeling. Tickets had sold out within hours, and the only reason Trinity had been able to get her hands on a few was because the organizers were clients. It probably also helped that LEPA would be providing security for the event.

A soft knock sounded at the door, and Connie pulled it open. She nodded at Jade, letting her know she could take it from there.

"Hi, Ms. Sanderson. Come on in. I'm Connie Shaw."

"Nice to meet you." The woman shook her hand. "And, please, call me Indie. Thanks for agreeing to see me on such short notice."

"No problem, and you can call me Connie."

Indie strolled farther into the office, looking every bit the statuesque beauty who probably booked photo shoots for three hundred dollars an hour.

"I love your outfit," Connie said of the white flowy jumpsuit belted at her tiny waist.

"Thank you." Her megawatt smile that was warm and genuine and showcased perfectly straight teeth lit up her face. Add those features to her flawless style, and it was no wonder why the woman was at the top of the modeling industry.

"All right, let's get started." Connie directed Indie to one of the guest chairs in front of the desk, while she reclaimed her seat behind the desk. "On the phone you mentioned that you needed personal security for the event."

"Yes. Tantanene's Jewelers referred me to you. I'd

like to have security while I'm in town. A bodyguard who can also serve as a driver."

"That won't be a problem," Connie said. LEPA had a fleet of vehicles, and most of their team were defensive-driving certified. It wasn't uncommon for their guards to take on double duty: provide security and be their client's drivers during the assignment.

"I'll be modeling some of Tantanene's jewelry during the fashion show Friday. But they are also lending me a couple of pieces that are valued at over half a million dollars to wear to an awards show in town next Saturday."

"Wow," Connie said, not meaning to say it aloud.

"Yeah, I know. It's quite an honor. That also means I'll be in town a little longer than anticipated, and I would like to hire LEPA's services for my entire stay."

"Sounds good." Connie logged on to her computer. "I received your list of criteria and have identified a few excellent choices."

She pulled up the file that contained the portfolios of those she had chosen and turned the screen so Indie could see. Their security team was comprised of men and women with impressive backgrounds. Most were college-educated and had some type of training in martial arts and hand-to-hand combat, or they were former military, and some were even law enforcement.

Connie pointed at one of the photos. "I think Randall would be a good—"

"Wait," Indie said. "Go back to the previous page."

Connie went back to the page with the photos of the twenty individuals she had selected.

"Is that Trace?" Indie said with awe in her voice and moved closer to the screen. "*Trace Halstead* works for you?"

*Crap.* Connie hadn't intended to include him in the lineup. He had requested time off from guarding, and Trinity had put him on a special assignment.

"Yes, Trace does work for the company, but unfortunately—"

A quick knock sounded at the door before it flew open.

"Connie, I checked the condo," Trace said before coming into view, but he pulled up short when he saw that she wasn't alone. "Oh, man, I'm sorry. I didn't realize you..." His words trailed off when his gaze landed on her visitor.

Connie was pretty sure Indie got that reaction from every man with just a heartbeat. And she probably should be jealous, but not even she could deny that the woman was beautiful.

But as Connie watched Trace, she knew something wasn't right. She stood and didn't miss the various emotions flashing across Trace's handsome features. Surprise. Confusion. Revulsion. Then his face twisted into an angry scowl.

"What the hell is *she* doing here?" he spit out, disgust dripping from each word.

Connie straightened, shocked by his outburst. He was always kind and professional, and this was a side of him she hadn't witnessed before. Whatever history he had with this woman definitely wasn't good.

# Chapter 12

Trace stood frozen. Just seeing Indie brought back painful memories of when they'd dated. He'd been a senior in high school when she'd taken him home to meet her parents and her father had told him that he wasn't good enough for his daughter. Mr. Sanderson had barely greeted Trace before ushering him into his massive home office. He wasted no time in telling Trace that not only wasn't he allowing Indie to go to prom with him, but he also didn't want him anywhere near her.

Trace could almost hear the conversation all over again.

*You'll never amount to anything.*

*You'll always be a nobody.*

*You're not even good enough to breathe the same air as her.*

Connie put her hands on her hips and glared at him. "I take it you know Ms. Sanderson."

"Yeah, I know her," he finally said. "Indie and I attended high school together."

Her father's words had crushed Trace. Now it was as if he was being taken back to that moment. The embarrassment, anger and failure he'd felt then returned with a vengeance, and his chest tightened. He balled his fists at his sides and glared at the woman he'd had no intention of ever seeing again.

But how was it possible that years-old devastation could still affect him now? He had given up. Stopped caring about anything and everything after that one-on-one with her father. Had it not been for his own father and Trace's siblings, there was no telling where Trace would've ended up. He'd been headed down a bad path that probably would've resulted in jail time or worse.

Now, seeing Indie again, Trace could almost envision the sneer on her father's face. The judgment. The hate. Edward Sanderson didn't bother hiding his dislike of him.

"I'm sorry, Indie. Trace is not available for your assignment," Connie said, her voice snapping him out of his trance. She had reclaimed her seat and was typing something into her computer. "I do have someone else who would be perfect. Here we go."

Connie turned the computer screen around, but Indie ignored it. Trace wasn't bothered by the way her gaze traveled the length of him. Her smoldering eyes consumed every inch, regarding him as if he was a double chocolate cupcake that she wanted to devour. As a matter of fact, it gave him pleasure to see interest in her eyes. He wanted her to see what she had missed out on.

"I don't want anyone else. I only want Trace," she said with authority. Her sultry voice, which probably made other men fall at her feet, had the opposite effect on him. Trace couldn't seem to shake the loathing running through his body.

"Why?" he asked Indie before Connie could respond. "Why would you want my protection when your father insisted that I'd never be good enough for you? That I shouldn't even be allowed to breathe the same air as you?" Anger bubbled inside him and he tried to tamp it down. He had to remember that it didn't matter how he felt about her—she was a potential client for LEPA.

"Seriously, Trace? That was a hundred years ago. Besides, that's what my father thought. Not me."

Trace loved his own father, the man who'd worked his ass off to keep a roof over their heads, but he had admired Mr. Sanderson. Like him, Trace had wanted to one day own some type of business and put his stamp on the world. So when the older man had raked him over the coals, it had done more than hurt his confidence—it had devastated him to the core.

He didn't say anything even though he could argue that fact. He didn't care if it had been a hundred years ago—his feelings for her and her family remained the same. He wanted nothing to do with any of them.

Without another word, he walked out of the office. He might've been acting like a complete jerk, and even though he knew Connie would ream him out later, Trace couldn't help himself.

Forty-five minutes later, Connie found him in the staff lounge. Most of the administrative staff had left for the day. Trace had stuck around, knowing that he and Connie would need to talk.

"You put on quite a show in there," she said as she walked farther into the room.

He gauged her demeanor. She didn't seem as annoyed as she had appeared in her office, and for that he was grateful. His gaze raked over her body, taking in the sexy outfit that sheathed her hourglass figure. Damn, she was fine. He loved when she wore dresses and skirts, giving him a chance to see her shapely legs.

"I'm sorry about what happened in there. I hope I didn't blow the deal."

Trace stood when Connie approached the table, and he pulled out a chair for her. She sat next to him but didn't say anything right away. Instead, she crossed her legs, causing her skirt to ride up and give him just enough of a peek of her toned thigh to make his dick twitch.

"Care to tell me what that was all about?"

Debating how much to tell her, Trace sipped the steaming coffee that he had made a few minutes ago.

"Did I ruin the deal?" he asked.

"No. She's still very interested in our services, even if she can't have you."

Trace studied Connie, not missing how possessive it sounded when she said "even if she can't have you." Maybe he was reading too much into her statement, but damn if it didn't feel good to have her in his corner. Especially when she didn't yet know the whole story.

"Indie actually said you had a right to be angry, even if you were acting childish." Connie lifted her eyebrows and a smile played on her ruby-red lips.

"Why do I have a feeling you added the 'childish' part?"

She shrugged. "Okay, maybe I did, but your attitude was way out of character in there. I take it that Indie was the prom date that you mentioned the other day."

"Yeah, but she and I didn't attend prom together. I'm sorry about my jacked-up behavior back in the office. I was *way* out of line. She might've caught me off guard, but I'll make it right with her."

Trace told Connie what had happened between him and Indie. Outside of his family and Maxwell, he had never shared the story with anyone. It hadn't been one of his favorite moments.

"I looked up to her father without even knowing the man. At the time, he'd been a part owner of a casino and very active at our school. Always showing up for various events, donating computers and tons of other stuff the school needed. I idolized the guy from a distance. He had a powerful presence about him. Always dressed to perfection, drove the sharpest cars, and I liked the way he carried himself—like a boss.

"I did all right academically in school," he admitted, "and had always been athletic, but I was a little shy."

"*You* were shy?" Connie asked, her mouth hanging open.

Trace chuckled. "I know it's hard to believe, but yeah. I was on the shy side. I was slowly starting to open up toward the end of my junior year. Mainly because the girls were sweating me and boosting my confidence."

Connie laughed. "I find it hard to believe that you weren't always confident and maybe a little arrogant."

Trace shook his head and grinned, but then turned serious. "Indie would always flirt with me, especially once we became seniors. She had hinted around about us attending prom together, but I knew my father didn't have money for me to go. I hadn't planned to go, but Indie was the most popular girl in school and her father was *the man.*

"With her by my side, I felt like the big man on campus, that I could be like him one day. Walking around with my chest stuck out because Indie, every boy's dream girl, was into me. She even wanted me to meet her parents."

Embarrassment stirred inside Trace as he mentally traveled down memory lane. He told Connie about how Indie had invited him over for dinner at her parents' estate. Wanting to make a good impression, Trace had borrowed his oldest brother's suit for the occasion. He couldn't wait to meet Mr. Sanderson. He even had a list of questions to ask about running his own business.

"Indie's father *crushed* me with his words. My hero, even though I didn't really know him, had destroyed my confidence with one conversation. After that, I didn't give a damn about anything. I did so much stupid shit, even to the point of *almost* getting expelled toward the end of my senior year. I was basically living up to all the crap Sanderson said about me."

Connie reached over and covered Trace's hand with

hers. "I can't even imagine how you must've felt. Even worse, it sickens me that an adult would talk to a child that way. He could've just told you that you couldn't date his daughter. He didn't have to break your pride the way he did. How'd you get your life back on track?"

"My dad. One night he picked me up from the police station after I had gotten into some trouble. On the way home, he told me that was a onetime *gift*. That if I ever got into trouble with the law again, I was on my own. Then I learned that Langston had told him about Mr. Sanderson."

"What did your dad say?"

Trace's heart swelled as he thought about his father, the man who'd basically saved his life. "He told me he loved me. That he would *never* stop loving me, but it was up to me to determine the type of life I wanted to live. He said as far as Sanderson was concerned, a *real* man would never tear down a young man. He also told me that I needed to do a better job at choosing my role models."

"That was wonderful advice. He sounds like a great dad."

"He's the best." The type of father Trace hoped to one day be. "He lives in the Bahamas now, but I look forward to introducing you to him one day."

Connie gave him a shy smile, and hope blossomed inside Trace.

"I look forward to it."

Now he was cheesing so hard, his cheeks hurt.

Connie crossed her legs. "I take it you got your act together after that."

"Well, it still took me a minute." Trace chuckled, thinking about a few more stupid incidents that he'd gotten himself into. "I joined the navy shortly after graduation, and it was the best decision for me. Between the training and life experiences while serving, I regained my confidence, earned my degree in business, and look at me now. I'm sitting here with the woman of my dreams."

"Oh, brother. There you go, tryin' to charm me again."

Trace brought her hand to his lips. "Is it working?"

Connie laughed and pulled back her hand. "Maybe a little."

Trace smiled, glad that he was wearing her down. "Does that mean that once your life settles down a little, you'll let me take you on a proper date?"

Her beautiful smile and the way her eyes glittered with adoration sent heat pulsing through his body. The last few days with her had confirmed it for him—he wanted her in his life.

Connie hadn't even agreed to date him, but deep in his heart, Trace knew she was the woman for him. She stirred something inside him, something he couldn't quite put a name to, but he loved the way it made him feel. He was a protector by nature, and even though she was ridiculously independent, she made him…feel. Needed. Adored. She made him feel as if he mattered in her life.

"Yes," Connie said quietly. "I'd love to go on a date with you."

For a minute, all Trace could do was stare at her. He

was so used to her saying no that he hadn't actually thought about how it would be when she finally said yes.

"Would you mind putting that in writing and getting it notarized? Just in case you conveniently forget when the time comes."

Connie burst out laughing, then stood and straightened her clothes. "I just can't with you."

"Baby, you can do anything you want with me. Just say the word. I'm all yours."

Trace's cell phone vibrated in his front pocket. As he stood, he pulled it out and read the text from Trinity.

Connie isn't answering her phone. Are you still at the office?

He typed back a quick response. Yes, and she's here.

Good. Come over for dinner and bring her with you. We need to talk.

Trace sent a thumbs-up emoji. It wasn't unusual for Trinity to invite him over, but this was the first time that she'd told him to bring Connie.

He glanced up at her. "The boss has summoned us to her house for dinner. Are you game?"

"Kinda late notice. Did she say why?"

"Only that we need to talk."

# Chapter 13

"Why do I have to be up to something?" Trinity asked Connie with a tad of defensiveness in her tone. "Maybe I just wanted to have my friends over for dinner."

They were in Trinity's massive kitchen preparing side dishes, while Trinity's husband, Gunner, and Trace were on the deck out back grilling.

Connie sliced the strawberries that would go into the fruit salad she was preparing. "Who invites people over to eat and then makes them cook? I assumed dinner would already be ready."

"Where's the fun in that? Besides, you and Trace aren't guests. You're family. This is what family does. We cook together. We eat together. We love on each other."

"Yeah, whatever. Next time you call us over here for

dinner, I expect it to already be prepared." Trinity set a bowl of green grapes, a cantaloupe and a fresh pineapple on the counter. "I can't wait to cut into the pineapple. I can already smell its sweetness."

Trinity popped a grape into her mouth and leaned against the counter. "So, you and Trace seem to be getting closer."

Connie didn't take the bait. Her friend had been trying to push the two of them together for a long time. Now that Connie was getting to know Trace better, she recognized Trinity might've been right. He was beyond what she'd expected, and she looked forward to spending more time with him.

"Okay, you don't have to tell me what's going on. I saw the way he looked at you before he headed outside. Or maybe I should say, the way he *ogled* you. I guess staying the weekend at his place was the turning point, huh?"

"Maybe. Is that why you called us over here, so you could pry into our personal lives?"

"I do not pry. If I want to know something, I just ask." Trinity grabbed the oven mitts and went to the stove to pull out a pan of baked ziti. "But, anyway, I called you two over because I've been thinking. Since you told me about the incident at Heavenly Sandwich Shop the other day, something has been on my mind. I have an idea, and before you say *no*, hear me out."

Connie started shaking her head before Trinity could say anything else. "Whatever it is, *no*. Every time you start out with 'before you say no,' I already know I'm not going to like whatever you're going to say."

"That's not true. Remember when I suggested you quit your job and join me at the agency? That hasn't turned out bad, and I started the conversation the same way."

*True.* Trinity's call had been a godsend. Before joining LEPA, Connie had helped her with administrative work on occasion, had even filled in a few times when other staff members were on vacation. She hadn't expected the job offer. Trinity called and practically begged her to consider working at LEPA, saying that she needed someone she could trust and depend on by her side.

The timing couldn't have been better. It was days after Connie's world imploded with Quincy's betrayal. She had taken some vacation time to pull herself together, time to expel the anger and hate that had consumed her. Connie knew she could no longer work for the marketing company. Had she stayed, Quincy would've been her boss. Trinity didn't know any of that before she called, which made Connie think that it was divine intervention at its best.

The door to the back deck slid open, and Trinity's three-year-old son strolled in with a teddy bear tucked under his arm. Connie smiled as her thoughts went immediately to the night she had told Trace that she still slept with her doll, Vinnie. She had to keep herself from laughing now as she remembered his reaction.

"Mommy, can I have a cupcake? *Ple-e-ease.*"

"Not before dinner, baby. How about a slice of apple?"

"Can I have apple *and* a cupcake?" Jonah tried bargaining, giving his mother the sweet puppy-dog eyes that he had mastered.

Connie didn't know how Trinity could say no to all of that cuteness. Jonah had the most beautiful eyes, and long, curled eyelashes that would make any woman jealous. He also had Gunner's disposition—sweet and mild-mannered. Their easygoing personalities were the opposite of Trinity's. She wasn't the most patient person.

"Nope, only apple right now." Trinity held out a slice, and Jonah stared at it with his eyebrows pulled together. He glared at the fruit as if it had the ability to bite him.

"But, Mommy, I don't want apples."

"All right, I guess that leaves more for me." Trinity ate the slice in two bites and returned to what she was doing. Jonah frowned at her but didn't say another word. He turned and headed to the family room. Seconds later, Connie heard the television, and the sound of his giggles drifted from the other room.

"You do know that this next child is probably going to have your personality, right?"

Trinity's shoulder slumped, and she leaned against the counter. "Yeah, and it scares me to death. Gunner wants a girl and that terrifies me even more."

"That would be so cool. Then you'll have a little Mini-Me," Connie gushed, thinking how she would love to have a little girl of her own. It was something she used to think about often, but after she and Quincy parted ways, that dream left with him. Until lately. The other night she had dreamed that she and Trace had gotten married, and she was pregnant with their first child.

Connie had woken up in his guest room, and hearing him bumping around in the condo made the dream seem that much more real.

"I don't think I can handle a Mini-Me," Trinity said, interrupting Connie's thoughts. "My mother often tells stories of how I was a little terror growing up. She also says that payback's a you-know-what." Trinity waved her hand as if dismissing the notion. "But, anyway, getting back to what we were talking about. I think you should consider keeping Trace around."

"If I agree with you, can we change the subject?"

Trinity narrowed her eyes. "I'm not sure because that was a little too easy. I had this great speech planned and you're ruining it."

Connie shook her head, laughing.

"But I will say this, sis. Trace adores you, and he's worried. We both are. So heads up—he's probably going to try planting himself into your life one way or another."

The doorbell rang before Connie could respond, and Trinity went to the door. Trace had already made it clear that he was around to stay, at least until the robbers were caught. Connie would be lying if she said that the incident at the restaurant hadn't shaken her a little. Yet she didn't want a bodyguard, or someone following her around 24/7. As for Trace being in her life for other reasons? Connie was warming up to that idea.

"Hey, baby girl," Maxwell said to Connie when he strolled into the kitchen with his arm looped around Trinity's shoulder. The brother and sister were a couple of years apart, but when they stood that close to each other, they could be twins. At over six feet tall and built like Trace, Maxwell was handsome with skin a deep shade of mahogany and a smile that could brighten the darkest day.

"Hey, yourself." Connie wiped her hands on a dish towel and moved around the counter to hug him. "Trinity didn't mention you were coming to dinner."

"I wasn't planning on it, but when I found out Trace was here, I figured I'd stop by." He held up a folded sheet of paper and glanced around. "Where is he? I have something for him."

"He's on the deck with Gunner."

"Uncle Max!" Jonah yelled. He tore out of the family room and leaped into Maxwell's arms.

"What's up, li'l man?"

"Nothing, but Mommy won't let me have a cupcake."

Maxwell laughed and tickled his nephew, who fell into a fit of giggles. "I guess I need to talk to that mommy of yours, huh?"

Jonah nodded vigorously. "Yes. Can you tell her to give me one? The yellow one?"

"Jonah, I'm not changing my mind," Trinity said simply and placed dinnerware and utensils on the counter. "Go see if Daddy is finished barbecuing."

After Maxwell walked out with Jonah in his arms, Connie and Trinity organized the food on the long center island.

"Before they come trampling in here, think about what I was saying. If you don't officially want personal security, at least continue hanging out with Trace.

I know he won't let anything happen to you, and it'll make me feel better knowing someone has your back."

Connie pulled the lemonade that Trinity had made earlier from the refrigerator and set it on the center island next to the glasses. "Did Trace put you up to this?"

"No, but he did ask my opinion. He wanted to know if I thought there was a chance you could be in danger."

Connie trusted her friend's instinct. "Do you? Do you think there's a possibility that those guys will realize that I saw part of one of their tattoos? Or that I worked with a sketch artist?"

"At first, I didn't really think so, but there's too much we don't know. Will the guy you made eye contact with remember what you look like? Like, you remember *his* eye color, but he might recall your hazel eyes. Does he have the ability and resources to find out who you are and hunt you down? Those are things no one knows."

Unease clawed through Connie, and she tried to steady her breathing. "I doubt he'd go to the trouble. I didn't see much of him."

"That's true. I didn't start to really get concerned until hearing about what happened at the restaurant. You know I don't believe in coincidences. You said the man's eye color was unusual and that his eyes looked familiar. Then you run into someone whose eyes are identical to the bank robber? Too much of a coincidence for me."

"Maybe, but I'm not a hundred percent sure about anything. Besides, I can't remember seeing a tattoo on the guy. So at this point, I don't trust my judgment or my memory."

"I get it. When I was a cop, we could interview ten

different people who claimed to have witnessed the same crime, and all ten would give different accounts. Everyone notices different things. That's just how it is."

"I guess, but it doesn't make me feel any better about this situation."

"That's okay. Right now, my main concern is that we're looking out for *you*. At least think about it. I'd rather you have someone by your side and not need them than to need them and not have anyone."

"All right, all right. I hope you ladies are ready," Gunner said when he hurried in with a large platter of meats. Jonah trailed behind him carrying tongs and a spatula.

"Looks like 'The Hunk' has done his cooking proud," Connie said, using the nickname she had given Gunner when he and Trinity first started dating. He wasn't much of a cook, but like many men, he was great on the grill. "It smells amazing."

"And it tastes even better," Gunner said, setting the food on the counter where Trinity had made space.

Connie's heart melted when he wrapped his arm around his wife and placed his hands on her small baby bump. Then he turned her and kissed her as if he hadn't seen her in days.

They were obnoxiously cute. Connie loved them both to death, and she hated to admit that sometimes she was jealous of their relationship. Trinity was living the life that Connie one day wanted. They made being married seem like so much fun while also making it look easy, though she knew it wasn't. Considering Trinity and Gunner's rocky start, though, Connie was glad to see that they were still madly in love. Gunner, a professional poker player who used to be Maxwell's college roommate, had hired LEPA a few years ago. A deadly criminal was taking out professional poker players, and Gunner was concerned for his safety. His two stipulations when hiring personal security: he wanted Trinity as his security specialist, and he needed her by his side around the clock. Not only had Trinity kept him safe, but they'd also fallen in love.

"Where's Max and Trace?" Trinity asked when the kiss ended. "I'm surprised they didn't follow you inside. I know they have to be hungry."

Gunner set a couple of bottles of beer next to the lemonade. "They were talking but said they'd be in shortly."

"Mommy, now can I have a cupcake?"

"Jonah, do not ask me that again. I already said that you couldn't have one before dinner, and I meant it. We're going to eat soon."

Trace and Maxwell strolled in, and Connie's gaze immediately landed on Trace. At first, he was frowning when he entered the kitchen, but the moment he saw her, he smiled and headed over to her. She didn't ever think she'd get used to the butterflies that took flight inside her stomach whenever he was near. Would it always be like that with him?

Trace pulled her to his side and placed a kiss on her temple as if it was the most natural thing to do. Connie's cheeks heated when she made eye contact with Trinity. Her friend was grinning like she had just been awarded a billion dollars.

Connie rolled her eyes and glanced up at Trace. "Ready to eat?"

"Definitely. I'm starving."

Once they were seated at the dining-room table, conversation flowed easily. That was always the case when Connie hooked up with Trinity and her family. But this was the first time that she was there with a man. Not just any man, but one who made her heart beat double time and her insides quiver.

She was done pushing him away. Done being afraid of getting hurt or making the wrong choice. Connie wanted...no, she deserved...to have the loving relationship she'd always dreamed of, and she could see that happening with Trace.

He squeezed her thigh, and Connie's pulse did a little giddyap. How was it possible that, with only a touch, this man could arouse the passion that had been dormant for too long inside her?

"You all right?" he asked close to her ear, his deep voice sending goose bumps spreading up her arms.

Connie glanced at him and smiled, something she'd been doing a lot of over the last few days. "I'm great." She noticed he had cleaned his plate. "Are you ready for dessert?"

His left eyebrow lifted in surprise and his lips quirked. She then realized how her question sounded.

"Cupcakes. I'm talking about cupcakes," she said quickly and a little louder than intended.

"Yay! We can have cupcakes," Jonah cheered at the other end of the table, where he was sitting next to

Gunner and across from Trinity. "Mommy, can I have a yellow one?"

Trinity pointed her fork at Connie. "The next time you bring cupcakes into this house, you better sneak them in."

Connie grinned at her friend. "I can't make any promises on that."

Everyone turned to Maxwell and Gunner, who were engaged in a heated discussion about basketball. The NBA playoff season was kicking off and Gunner insisted that the Lakers were going to win the title.

"Actually, the Lakers are playing tonight. I just can't remember what time," Trace said.

Gunner strolled into the family room, where they had the biggest television Connie had ever seen hanging on the wall. He scrolled through a few channels. "They're probably on now."

"Stop!" Trace yelled and jumped out of his seat before Connie could figure out what was going on. "Go back."

Gunner flipped back to the previous channel and stopped on a news station. He turned up the volume.

Connie stood slowly, and unease crept through her body when she recognized the photo on the television screen. She walked over and stopped in the middle of the room next to Trace.

*"According to authorities, a woman's body was found at the West Meadow Inn motel. The woman, who sustained a single gunshot wound to the head, has been identified as Janel Landrey, age twenty-eight. She was the bank teller at Sunburst Bank for whom au-*

*thorities have been searching in connection with the
recent robbery. Her death is being ruled a homicide.
The bank robbers are still at large and should be considered armed and dangerous. They are wanted for the
murder of Richard Holmes and also are suspects in the
murder of Ms. Landrey. There's a fifty-thousand-dollar
reward for information leading to the apprehension of
these individuals. If you have any information..."*

Connie didn't hear the rest as she stood frozen. All
she could think about was how they had shot the woman
in cold blood. *Her* bank teller. A gunshot to the head.
What type of heartless people would do something like
that to another human being? She might not have known
or even have ever seen Janel until the day of the robbery, but her heart ached for the woman and those she'd
left behind.

"Connie," Trace said, his voice raised as if he had
already called her name several times. He was standing directly in front of her, and the worry radiating in
his eyes made her stomach drop. He cupped her face
between his hands and moved closer, their noses almost
touching. "I don't know what's going on in that pretty
little head of yours, but nothing's going to happen to
you," he said, his voice only loud enough for her to hear.

She nodded. The conviction in Trace's voice helped
settle her nerves. One thing was for sure, though. Until
all of this was over, she was glad he would be by her side.

# Chapter 14

Days later, Connie stood in front of the full-length mirror hanging on the wall near her walk-in closet. She almost didn't recognize herself. For the first time in days, she felt physically good. No aches. No swelling. No stinging from scraped skin.

It was the night of the celebrity fashion show, and Connie had just slipped into her dress, which Trinity had talked her into buying a few weeks ago when they'd gone shopping. She twisted and turned in front of the mirror, loving the way the lightweight, flowy material moved. The pearl-white, backless outfit had a plunging neckline and hit just above her knees. It was definitely bolder than she would normally wear, but now that she was planning to attend with Trace, she was glad she had purchased it.

She turned one more time, glancing over her shoulder. "Damn, I look hot." She giggled, unable to help herself. The squats and lunges that she had incorporated into her workout were definitely paying off. Her butt looked incredible, if she did say so herself. Trace's eyes were going to fall out of his head when he saw her in the dress.

The thought made her grin harder, but it probably wasn't a good idea to tempt her bodyguard. As she double-checked her makeup, Connie thought about how much she was really enjoying having Trace by her side. It didn't feel like he was there to protect her. It was more like they were dating, which was fine with her. She was getting tired of skirting her attraction to him. It was time to let down her guard and allow their relationship to progress organically. She knew there'd be moments when her nerves would get the best of her. Not because of her feelings for Trace, but because the bank robbery and the subsequent murder were still plaguing her mind.

Trinity's brother, Maxwell, had looked into the case and found out that Janel had been planning to turn herself in to authorities. According to her, one of the robbers was an ex-boyfriend who'd been blackmailing her into helping him. She had two semesters of nursing school left, and he had threatened to send a sex tape that she hadn't known he'd made to the dean of her college.

According to Maxwell, Janel had never expected anyone to get hurt during the robbery. She panicked and ran when she learned that law enforcement knew of her involvement. Afraid her ex would find her before the cops, she agreed to turn herself in. Unfortunately, it seemed the criminals got to her before she could give the detectives on the case any names.

After leaving Trinity and Gunner's house the other night, Trace had stopped home and packed a bag. He'd stayed with Connie every night since then, and she was glad that he didn't seem to mind. They'd gotten into a good rhythm while sorta-kinda living together. They hadn't shared a bed since that first night at his place, but they'd shared plenty of kisses.

Connie glanced at the clock on the nightstand and gasped. They needed to head out; she didn't want to miss the preshow cocktail party and dancing before the fashion show.

She slipped into her four-inch strappy sandals, grabbed her small, bejeweled purse and wrap, then left the bedroom. The house was quiet, but she knew Trace was there somewhere.

Connie made her way to the living room and pulled up short. Her breath caught in her throat at the sight before her.

"Wow" was all she could say when her gaze landed on Trace leaning against the fireplace mantel. He looked like a *GQ* cover model ready for his next photo shoot. The man was already gorgeous on any given day, but seeing him in a black, satin-lapel tuxedo was like looking at a Nubian prince.

Her gaze traveled back up his body and took in every detail of her date for the evening. The cut of the tuxedo emphasized his broad shoulders and the way his body tapered down to a narrow waist. He was over six feet tall, but his legs seemed even longer in the tuxedo pants with satin stripes down the sides. Trace might've had confidence issues back in high school, but right now, he appeared poised and in charge.

"You are absolute perfection," Connie finally said.

Trace straightened and was checking her out the way she had just done to him. "And you're sexy as hell. Damn, girl. I'm going to be spending all my time tonight fighting off brothas who'll be trying to step to you."

Connie waved him off. "Oh, please. With the gorgeous models on center stage strutting their stuff, ain't nobody gon' be thinking about me."

"I disagree." Trace walked in a circle around her and cursed under his breath when he saw the back of the dress. "You're absolutely stunning, but this dress, though…"

Connie tried to fight the smile that was threatening to burst free, but she couldn't. She loved his reaction.

"Are you ready to go?" she asked.

"Yeah, the car should be here in a few minutes." Trace checked his phone.

They were using a car service to get to the event. There had been a recall on the power-steering package on his car, so his Camaro was in the shop. And since they planned to have a couple of drinks, it was better that they didn't drive, anyway.

In the morning, she was going to pack a few clothes to take to his place. Trace wanted her to stay with him until the bank robbers were caught, and Connie had agreed. She loved his condo. The security was great, and the weekend she'd stayed with him felt like being at a retreat of sorts.

Now that she had decided to break her rule about not dating coworkers, Connie was looking forward to her and Trace getting even closer. She was tired of trying to keep their relationship platonic when what she really wanted was him naked and in her bed again. Her sex-starved body hummed with anticipation of the night to come.

"The car will be here in three minutes. Do you have everything?" he asked.

"Yes. Before we go, we should probably talk about Indie. You're not going to make a scene tonight, are you?" Connie asked, knowing she sounded like someone's mother instead of a date.

Technically, this wasn't a date. Trace was just escorting her to the event, but in Connie's heart, this was going to be their first date. And she wanted to make sure it was perfect.

"I promise I won't make a scene, and I won't embarrass you. Hopefully, I'll see Indie and get a chance to apologize for the other day."

"As long as that's all you do," Connie said as she straightened his tie. "Don't forget—tonight you're mine."

Trace's tempting lips twisted into a sexy grin, and he looped his arm around her waist. "You know I love it when you talk dirty."

Connie burst out laughing. "Only you would consider that talking dirty."

"Maybe, but still, I liked the way it sounded, and don't worry. I'm all yours and not just for tonight." He lowered his head and covered her mouth with his, and Connie's toes curled inside her high heels as she gave herself freely to the slow, drugging kiss. She would never get enough of this strong, sexy man who had her panting even after their lip-lock ended. "Now, let's get out of here so that I can go and show you off looking all sexy in that dress."

Connie couldn't help the smile that spread across her face. "All right, if you insist."

Twenty minutes later, they arrived at the convention center. The event had been advertised as being one of the premier shows of the year. From what Connie could see so far, it was going to be spectacular.

While Trace talked to a couple of the security guys on duty who worked for LEPA, Connie glanced around. This was her first celebrity fashion show, and she took in every detail. The beautifully decorated ballroom was large and had black-and-gold gossamer fabric draped from the ceiling, giving the space a whimsical ambience.

The oversize room was playing double duty. On one side, a long, elevated runway covered in red carpet. Large gold stars, like those on the Hollywood Walk of Fame, ran down the center of it and took up much of the space. Clear, twinkling lights going around the outer edge lit the space. Hundreds of chairs were set up on both sides of the platform, but the area was roped off, since the show didn't start until eight o'clock. The show's theme was Old Hollywood, and not only would the models be dressed accordingly, but the decor was befitting with oversize movie reels, old-fashioned film strips and vintage spotlights strategically placed in the area.

On the other side of the ballroom were four cash bars and at least forty tall cocktail tables. They were strategically placed around the large dance floor in the center of the space. Waiters, dressed in tuxedos, carried trays of bite-size hors d'oeuvres and floated about seamlessly. And a live band, set up on the side of the room, played soft jazz and added to the magical atmosphere.

Though Trinity and Gunner called to say that they wouldn't be able to attend, Connie was glad she and Trace were there. He approached her from behind and slid an arm around her waist.

"How about we get a drink? Or would you like to dance first?"

Connie couldn't wait to dance with him but opted for a drink first. "What do you think so far?" Trace asked when he handed Connie a glass of white wine. "It looks like no expense was spared in pulling all of this together."

"I agree. I'm already impressed with what I've seen. I can only imagine how great the show will be."

For the next few minutes, they talked, laughed and mingled with others. What she was enjoying most, though, was her time with Trace. Being with him reminded Connie of how long it had been since she'd been out with a man. She could honestly admit that no other compared to Trace. He was attentive, funny and sociable. It amazed her how many people he knew in attendance. Even with that, he hadn't left her side and treated her as if she was a precious gift.

Would it always be like that with him? Connie imagined it would be, and that only made her look forward to their relationship growing.

"Dance with me," Trace said and took her almost empty wineglass from her hand, setting it on a nearby table. "I don't want this evening to end without having you in my arms."

Connie smiled, and her pulse quickened at the idea of being hugged up against him. "I'd love to dance with you."

Trace grasped her hand, and they wove around small groups of people and tables as he guided her to the dance floor. Once they were there, the band started playing Percy Sledge's "When a Man Loves a Woman." There were two lead singers, but only the man was currently performing. Connie felt each note deep in her soul. He crooned the words with such passion and power, it was as if he was singing directly to his lover.

Trace gently pulled Connie into his arms and against his hard body. He held one of her hands to his chest, while his other arm slid around her waist. He rested that hand on the bare skin of her back just above her butt. Every nerve inside her body came alive, and a shiver scurried across her heated skin.

Being hugged up against him had an effect on her that defied all understanding, and *man*, he smelled amazing. Connie inhaled deeply, savoring Trace's hypnotic fragrance. Then she released the breath slowly as their bodies swayed to the smooth melody.

"Our first dance," Trace whispered close to her ear. His warm breath sent heat shooting across her skin.

Connie leaned her head back slightly and gazed into his eyes. "I'm never going to forget this dance. Or the song that we're dancing to."

"Good, because I'm thinking that it'll be the song we use for the first dance at our wedding reception."

Connie sputtered a laugh. "Aren't you being a little presumptuous? How do you know I'd ever agree to marry you?"

"Oh, I know. One day, baby. It's going to be me and you. I don't know when, but it's going to happen. You'll see."

"You sound awfully sure of yourself."

"I am. You're it for me."

Trace lowered his head and covered her mouth with his. His demanding lips caressed hers in a slow, heady kiss that sang through her veins. This man. God, this sweet, endearing, sexy man set her body on fire and stoked the flames with each lap of his tongue. He crushed her to him, deepening their lip-lock, and Connie savored him and the moment they were creating.

This wasn't just any kiss. This was a kiss from a man who was claiming her as his own. There was a time that would have scared her, but not now. Joy soared through Connie's veins and danced inside her at the thought of her and Trace together. *For real* together. Not just hanging out and going way past just a friendship.

It wasn't until the kiss ended that she remembered that they were in the middle of a dance floor. She didn't care. All she cared about in that moment was that she was with a man she absolutely adored. That wall that she had carefully constructed around her heart—gone. She was his.

Connie laid her head against Trace's shoulder as they continued swaying, now to a different song. A smile covered her lips, and her imagination took her down that road of…what if. What if their relationship grew to the point of marriage? What if they were able to build the life—together—that she had always dreamed of having?

It was way too soon to think along those lines, but right now, there was no other man she could imagine herself being with.

His to Protect

# Chapter 15

"I accept your apology, Trace, but it wasn't necessary," Indie said. She was standing in front of him, in the middle of a private hallway, in a short kimono robe and hair rollers.

Even looking the way she was, she was still as pretty as she was in high school. Yet Trace felt nothing. No longing. No attraction. Nothing. He knew why. It was because Connie owned his heart.

Working for the company providing security for the event definitely had its advantages. After making sure one of their guys was keeping an eye on Connie, Trace had made his way to the restricted area. Only the models and the production crew were allowed back here, and he was glad he'd been able to catch Indie before the show.

"The apology was definitely necessary," he said. "I was way out of line at the office the other day, taking my issues with your father out on you. I'm glad it didn't affect your choice in hiring LEPA, since they are the best security firm in the state."

Her million-dollar smile made an appearance. "That's what I heard, and so far, I'm very satisfied. As for my father, he ran every boy away, claiming that no one was good enough for his daughter. I knew there had been a conversation, but I didn't know exactly what was said."

"He didn't tell you?"

"No. Trace, when I invited you to dinner, I wanted them to meet you. You were such a nice guy. I thought for sure they'd let me go to prom with you. After you left, me and my dad had it out, but he wouldn't tell me what he had said to you. Then when I tried talking to you at school, you ignored me."

Trace shoved his hands into his pockets, remembering how he had cut her loose. The moment he walked out of her parents' home, he'd been done with them and her.

He glanced down at his black patent-leather lace-ups before returning his attention to her. "I definitely didn't handle that situation well. But like you said, that was a hundred years ago. So how's your dad doing?"

After leaving the military, Trace had thought about looking up Sanderson many times. He wanted to show the man how he had turned out. That despite what Sanderson had said to him that day, he had made something of himself.

"Well, after losing his and my mother's life savings with gambling, he died in a car accident seven years ago."

"Oh, wow." He might've despised the guy, but he hadn't wished him dead. "I'm sorry for your loss."

Indie shrugged with a sad smile. "It was a long time ago."

The door to the dressing area opened, and a woman with shocking red hair stuck her head out. "Two minutes, Indie."

"Okay, I'll be right there." Indie turned back to Trace. "It was good seeing you again. I hate the way things ended between us, but I was young and... Anyway, I'm sorry for everything my father said to you that day. More than anything, I'm glad you were able to prove him wrong."

"Yeah, me, too. Well, I'll let you finish getting ready. Thanks for giving me a minute and good luck with the show."

"Thanks, and you take care of yourself. Oh, and here's my number." She handed him a small slip of paper that she pulled from the pocket in the robe. "In case... well, just in case." Trace nodded and walked away. He glanced at the name and digits on the paper, then shoved it into his pocket. He had no intention of ever calling Indie, but he was glad to close that chapter of his life.

An hour and a half later, during intermission, Trace brought his glass of whiskey to his lips and took a sip. For much of the night, he hadn't been able to take his attention off Connie. When she'd first mentioned wanting to attend the fashion show, he hadn't thought it was a good idea. Especially after hearing that the criminals had gotten to Janel Landrey.

That murder didn't sit well with Trace on so many levels. Shooting someone point-blank in the head meant that these weren't just some young punks who had robbed the bank. His guess would be that they were part of a gang or another organized-crime syndicate. Maxwell had followed through on getting him a copy of the sketch of the tattoo that Connie had seen. Unfortunately, it wasn't enough to narrow down whether it could be a gang or prison mark. He just hoped that Connie wasn't on that man's radar.

Trace continued watching her as she stood a few feet away chatting with a client who had used LEPA's services in the past. His woman looked fierce and hella sexy in the white outfit, and, yes, after tonight, he was claiming her as his.

Then there was that kiss that they'd shared on the dance floor. Damn if he wasn't still feeling the intensity of that moment. After the kiss had ended, he'd wanted to scoop her up, toss her onto his shoulder and carry her to the nearest coatroom or closet. As recent as a couple of days ago, he had told himself that he would let her set the pace for their relationship, but now...

Trace slammed back the rest of the dark liquor in his glass, hoping it would help settle down his libido. The woman had a way of twisting him up inside and making him yearn for what they'd shared a little over a month ago. Once the fashion show was over, he planned to love on her luscious body until she screamed his name over and over again.

Trace glanced at his watch. There was still about ten minutes left of the intermission, and he was ready for the organizers to start the second half. Fashion shows weren't really his thing, but Connie seemed to be enjoying herself. That was most important to him. Then again, he had to admit that the show was better than he'd expected.

Trace looked up and saw Riley, one of the security specialists, trying to get his attention. Riley gave him a slight head nod, informing him to look to his left. They had worked enough assignments together to communicate without words. Whatever his friend was trying to warn him about wasn't good.

Trace glanced in the area indicated and groaned.

*Sylvia.*

If he was lucky, maybe she wouldn't see him. No sooner had the thought filtered into his mind than she glanced his way.

*That's just great.*

With that megawatt smile that had first attracted him to her, she strutted toward him like one of the models walking the runway. Nobody could deny that she was a beautiful woman, dressed in an evening gown similar to one that had been modeled earlier. Trace shouldn't have been surprised that she was there, as a self-proclaimed fashionista.

"Trace," she said in a singsong voice. "Why didn't you tell me you were planning to attend? We could've come together."

She lifted up to kiss him, but he turned his head at the last second and managed to dodge her lips.

"Hey, Sylvia," he said coolly, not missing the look of hurt on her perfectly made-up face.

She put her hand on her narrow hip. "Oh, so it's like that, huh?"

"It is, and we've already talked about this. You and me? We're done. Besides, I'm here with someone."

At that moment, Connie's gaze met his. An involuntary smile spread across Trace's mouth, and his body reacted immediately upon seeing her walking toward him.

His pulse amped up and he couldn't take his eyes off Connie. Watching her, the way her hips swayed—left, then right, then left again in that too-sexy-to-be-legal dress—was everything. He liked that the outfit was short, giving him a spectacular view of her gorgeous legs. Legs that had been wrapped around him before. Legs he wanted to get in between as soon as…

*Ah, hell. Down, boy.*

He needed to get a hold of himself before he embarrassed them both.

"Hey, sweetheart," he said once Connie was close enough to hear him. He lifted his arm and she stepped into his embrace, hugging up to him as if it was the most natural thing to do. If Trace had his way, he would never let her go.

"I want to introduce you to a friend of mine. Connie, this is Sylvia Turner. Sylvia, this is Connie Shaw, my date for the evening."

Trace wanted to say "his woman," but figured he was already pushing it by telling Connie he planned to marry her one day. She might've thought he was kidding, but he meant every word that he'd said to her on the dance floor.

"It's a pleasure to meet you, Sylvia. I've heard a lot about you."

Sylvia's brow lifted inquiringly as she shook Connie's hand. "Oh? I hope it was all good."

"It was," Connie said, not missing a beat. Trace hadn't told her much of anything about Sylvia. He wasn't sure why she'd said he had, but he was glad for the little white lie because Sylvia was eating it up.

"Your dress is gorgeous," she said to Connie, looking as if she meant every word.

"Thank you."

Sylvia tilted her head and glanced between him and Connie. Trace knew immediately that the questions were about to start.

"So, how long have you two been seeing each other?" Sylvia asked.

"It's been a while," Connie said and smiled up at Trace. She slipped her hand into his and squeezed. "The second half of the show is about to start, honey. Maybe we should reclaim our seats."

Trace could've kissed her in that moment. He knew Sylvia well enough to know that one question would've turned into thirty.

"Good idea, babe. And, Sylvia, it was good seeing you again. Take care and enjoy the rest of the show."

Trace directed Connie away without giving Sylvia a chance to say anything else. To Connie, he whispered, "I owe you one."

"And I intend to collect…tonight." Her saucy words

and her seductive grin sent all types of erotic thoughts racing through his mind.

As far as Trace was concerned, they could leave now. He was definitely ready to get out of there and pay his debt to her. How many times had he dreamed about them doing the horizontal tango again? Too many times to count. Now all he had to do was sit through the second half of the show without torturing himself with thoughts of how many different ways he planned to make her come.

For the next hour, they watched one model after another strut down the runway. There were ten minutes left in the show when Indie walked out modeling another outfit. It was her fifth or sixth wardrobe change, and with each one, she was stunning. This time she glided down the runway in a satin evening gown in pearl white with long matching gloves. She moved with such grace, keeping beat with the dramatic classical music that was playing.

A male model strutted alongside her. He wore a three-piece suit with a trench coat thrown over his arm and a cigarette dangling from his lips. Humphrey Bogart he wasn't, but Trace had to give it to the model for getting into character. Besides that, the suit was sharp. Dark in color, maybe a deep navy or charcoal black, it had a small check pattern and crisp lines, making the outfit appear that it had been tailored specifically for this guy.

Connie jerked next to him, pulling his attention from the stage. When he glanced at her, the startled expression on her face and the tension in her body had Trace sitting up straight.

"What's wrong?" he asked, loud enough for only her to hear. Placing his arm around her shoulders, he pulled her against his body. Unease clawed through him and his concern increased as she trembled and stared straight ahead.

"It—it's *him*," she said, her breaths coming in short spurts.

Trace followed her line of vision, and all he saw was Indie and the male model twisting and turning rhythmically together in some sort of dance, maybe a waltz.

"It's him," Connie said again, just as the models released each other and turned in Trace's direction.

That was when he saw it. The eyes. Gray eyes. If he wasn't mistaken, the man looked directly at Connie. He seemed just as stunned as she was before he strutted off the stage with Indie.

*Okay, this is some crazy sh—*

"Oh-my-god, oh-my-god, oh-my-god," Connie whispered as she squeezed Trace's thigh. When her fingernails started digging into his leg through the tuxedo material, he covered her hand with his.

"All right, baby, just breathe."

He glanced around for the nearest exit and tried to decide if they should make a move or sit tight for the next couple of minutes. They were in the third row, dead center. The chairs were so close together. If they stood up now, they'd definitely disturb a few people and draw attention to themselves. The grand finale was scheduled to begin in a few minutes, when all of the models would return to the stage, and hopefully he'd catch another glimpse of the man with the gray eyes.

With his arm still around Connie, Trace glanced down at her again. Her hand rested on her chest while she breathed in and out slowly.

"Are you okay?"

She nodded vigorously and continued regulating her breathing.

"I'm thinking we should wait before getting up. All right?" he asked.

She met his gaze. "That'll be fine. Sorry I freaked."

Trace gave her a quick peck on the lips, then eased his cell phone from his pants pocket. Since he didn't want to release Connie, he used his free hand to shoot Riley a text. Once the show ended, he wanted Noah, a member of LEPA's security team, to keep an eye on Connie, and Trace wanted Riley to meet him in the restricted area that the models were using.

Trace's attention returned to Connie. She had settled down but leaned limply against him.

During the grand finale, all of the models, at least fifty of them, paraded back onto the platform. But there was only one person he was interested in.

It took a few minutes before Trace spotted the man in question. Problem was, he was on the other side of the platform, facing opposite of where he and Connie were sitting.

Trace sent an additional text to Riley.

Don't let any models leave the building.

# Chapter 16

Trace paced the length of the small room designated for the security team like a caged animal. At first, he had considered hanging out in the hallway where he and Indie had chatted earlier, but then he thought better of that idea. At least this would give him a chance to talk to the gray-eyed model in private. That was assuming Riley could get him to the room without causing a scene.

Trace wasn't sure what he was going to say to the guy, but he had questions. Questions he hadn't quite formulated in his head, but he needed to determine if the man was a threat to Connie. Mr. Gray Eyes being at the restaurant and then the fashion show—those coincidences were too convenient for Trace's liking.

"Care to tell me what this is all about?" Hudson, another LEPA security specialist, asked. "Or at least let me know if I'm in here to keep you from laying hands on someone. Or to keep someone from laying hands on you."

"Hopefully, neither. I thought it was a good idea to have backup…for whatever goes down. I just want to talk to one of the models who keeps showing up wherever Connie is."

Connie hadn't been happy about him meeting with the guy, especially since she wasn't sure he was the one she'd seen at the bank. Trace had made it clear that all he wanted to do was feel the guy out and ask a few questions. If he suspected anything, they'd get the Feds involved.

"Hold up." Hudson pushed away from the wall that he'd been leaning against. "Connie has a stalker? Why didn't we know about this?"

"No, she doesn't have a stalker," Trace said. "At least as far as we know."

Connie had decided from day one that she didn't want the LEPA team, aside from Trinity and Trace, to know about the bank situation. As for her and Trace being together all the time, no one questioned it. There'd been a couple of guys he'd been on assignment with who speculated that he and Connie were an item. Trace never confirmed or denied, but he hadn't made it a secret that he was interested.

A few weeks ago, Riley had wished him luck with Connie, but threatened to kick his ass if he hurt her. Neither would ever happen because Trace had no intention of ever hurting her.

A quick knock sounded on the door before it opened, and Riley ushered in the model. Trace sized up the guy. The man was taller than he'd appeared while modeling, maybe six-two or six-three. They might've been close in height, but Trace had him by at least thirty pounds.

The gray-eyed man looked from Riley, to Trace, to Hudson. Then he returned his attention to Trace. "What's going on here?"

Trace folded his arms across his chest and studied the man whose eyes were similar to the sketch Connie had helped with. "That's what I'd like to know. Who are you?"

Trace could easily get his name from the fashion-show organizers and forward it to the Feds. But he wanted a face to face with the guy, especially after Connie's reaction. Seeing the way she freaked had Trace's protective instincts kicking into overdrive. Besides all of that, technically, the guy was just a model minding his own business. What Trace didn't want to do was have an innocent man get harassed by FBI agents for no reason.

The model glanced around again. He didn't appear to be bothered by the fact that three huge men were staring him down as if he had stolen something. Even Hudson's signature stare-down didn't seem to faze him.

That spoke volumes. Either the man was too stupid to be afraid, or he thought he could take all of them if anything broke out.

"I don't know what's going on here, but unless one of you tells me why I've been summoned, I'm out."

There was a commotion on the other side of the closed door, seconds before it swung open. A thick silence fell over the room when Connie appeared in the doorway.

Noah stood behind her with his hands out in front of him. "I tried to stop her, but…" He shrugged off the rest of the statement.

Without speaking a word, she slowly entered, her gaze steady on Mr. Gray Eyes. Noah closed the door and stayed in the hallway.

Trace sighed. So much for trying to keep Connie away from this man.

"I thought that was you. The hottie from the restaurant," Mr. Gray Eyes said and moved toward Connie until Trace blocked his path.

Now that he was in the man's face, Trace sensed that there was more to this guy. Something felt off. He couldn't pinpoint exactly what, but the uneasiness stirring in his gut was getting stronger by the minute. And he always trusted his gut.

"Do you know her?" Trace asked. He hated the way the man was leering at Connie. Like he desired her.

"I've seen her around," he said in a noncommittal tone.

The possessiveness Trace was feeling for Connie was almost suffocating. By nature, he was a protector. Not a fighter. But for her, he'd destroy anyone who caused her harm or even thought about hurting her.

"What's your name?" Trace asked, trying to keep his head. He wanted to put his fist in the man's face for the way he was still ogling Connie.

Mr. Gray Eyes seemed to grow taller right before Trace's eyes.

"Never mind who I am. Who are you, and what is this about?" He glanced at Connie. "This is the second time I've seen this fine-ass woman in a week. Each time, she looks at me like she's imagining me naked." His gaze took in the length of Connie, and he licked his lips before his eyes met Trace's. "Maybe she is. If you can't handle her, I'd be glad to show her what a real man—"

Trace didn't even feel himself move. All he knew was one minute he was trying to get information, and the next, he had the model pinned to the wall.

Connie gasped.

The gray-eyed man's eyes widened in surprise before they turned deadly.

Riley and Hudson must have anticipated Trace's move. They were at his side within a heartbeat. Neither said a word, but they didn't back away, either.

Anger boiled inside Trace while he had his forearm to the man's throat. Not hard enough to suffocate him, but hard enough to keep him plastered against the wall.

"Get. Off. Of. Me," the man said from between gritted teeth.

What surprised Trace, though, was that Mr. Gray Eyes didn't try to get out of his grasp. He kept his arms to his sides as he glared at Trace, a murderous look in his eyes.

"Who are you?" Trace asked, keeping the same amount of pressure on the man's throat.

"You can call me John Doe. I'm the man who is going to press charges and make sure you get arrested for aggravated assault if you don't release me."

Connie came up beside Trace and touched his arm. "Let him go." She took a giant step back. Maybe she knew he wouldn't release the guy while she was standing close to him.

"Stay away from her," Trace said, his voice low and lethal as he applied a little more pressure against the man's throat, "or I will make you sorry you ever looked at her."

"Release him," Connie said again, authority in her tone.

Trace reluctantly dropped his arm from the guy's throat, then stood next to Connie. The man slumped forward, his hands on his knees as he coughed a few times. When he was done, he slowly stood to his full height and straightened the suit jacket he was wearing.

"I don't know who you are or what your problem is, but put your hands on me again—" the model pointed a finger at Trace "—and you'll regret the day you ever came near me. I promise you that."

Trace didn't scare easily, and though he didn't feel threatened by the words, there was hardness in the man's eyes that gave Trace pause. He'd seen that look often enough during his combat days. This guy might appear harmless, but he had a feeling there was more to him than what they could see.

John Doe turned his attention to Connie. His appreciative gaze traveled down her body and back up again. To Connie's credit, she didn't wither under his stare. She stood her ground, looking fierce and sexy at the same time.

The man took his time shuffling backward toward

the door. Then he opened it, but didn't walk out. Instead, he glanced over his shoulder and pinned Connie in place with his eyes. Then he blew her a kiss. "Until we meet again…" With that, he was gone.

"I'm going to *kill* him." The words were out of Trace's mouth before he could pull them back, but he meant it. He released a long, unsteady breath, feeling as if he'd been submerged under water for an hour, and then suddenly his head was above the surface.

"Okay, will one of you tell me what the heck is going on?" Riley snapped.

Trace shook his head. "The hell if I know."

There was only one thing he knew for sure. He would continue to be Connie's shadow for the foreseeable future.

# *Chapter 17*

A half hour later, they strolled into Connie's house and she disarmed the security system. For the last few days, it seemed as if she'd been walking through a nightmare and couldn't wake up.

*What a night*, she thought.

The fashion show had been spectacular. Being with Trace was like a dream come true. Even dressing up and mingling with clients and others she'd just met had been fun. Not until she spotted Mr. Gray Eyes onstage did the evening start to fall apart.

Never in a million years did she think she'd see him again, especially in a matter of days. At first, when he strutted down the catwalk, Connie thought her eyes were playing tricks on her. It wasn't until he looked dead at her that she'd almost had a heart attack. Even then, though, she wasn't a hundred percent sure who she was seeing—the guy at the bank or the one from the restaurant. For all she knew, they were one and the same.

Connie glanced at Trace. He had just shrugged out of his tuxedo jacket and draped it on the back of one of the dining-room chairs. Now he was tugging on his bow tie, looking deep in thought.

He hadn't said much on the way back. Yet he'd stuck to her like a second skin. Riley, who had one of the company's cars, had driven them home. While they rode in the back seat, Trace held on to her hand. He acted like if he released her, she'd run away.

For a while there, she thought maybe he was pissed that she hadn't followed his instructions. The plan had been for her to stay with Noah while Trace talked to the mystery man. But right now, that didn't seem to be what was bothering him. He was working out something in his head. No surprise there. The last few days had given them both a lot to think about.

She had never seen Trace as angry as he'd been in that back room. Granted, she saw how upset he was when he ran into Indie the other day, but that was different. That day Connie had witnessed Trace in pain. Tonight, though, she saw a different side to him. There was no telling what he would've done to Mr. Gray Eyes had she not asked him to let the guy go.

Just thinking about the model's creepiness had her trembling inside. He might've been good-looking, but he was a little scary at the same time. It had been a tense few minutes, standing there with him inspecting her. Trace had just about lost his mind.

"I'm sorry about tonight," Connie said. "I should've waited with Noah as instructed. I wasn't thinking about the risk I could be in or the compromising position I put you and the other guys in."

"You have nothing to apologize for. I might've over-reacted, but seeing the man leering at you did something to me."

Under other circumstances, Connie would've been flattered to have Trace defending her honor. However, this situation made her uncomfortable on so many levels. She never wanted to be the cause of him getting hurt. Nor did she ever want to be the reason he got into trouble with the law.

"He didn't have a tattoo. At least not one I could see," Trace said, squinting as if trying to remember something. "The guy at the bank—where exactly was his tat?"

"You don't believe me, do you?" Connie asked.

Trace's eyebrows drew together. "What?" He tossed the bow tie onto the table and strolled over to where she was standing in the kitchen. "Sweetheart, of course I believe you. Why would you even doubt that?"

Connie sighed and reached up and fumbled with the French barrette that was holding up her hair. Once she removed it, her long curls fell in layers around her shoulders.

"Because I'm starting to question what I thought I saw at the bank. The only thing I'm a hundred percent sure of is that the robber had the most unusual gray eyes I have ever seen. Like the guy tonight."

Trace studied her for a long minute, then cupped her

cheek and brushed the pad of his thumb over her skin. His tenderness with her, and his ability to awaken her senses, always caught her off guard. In a good way.

She leaned into his touch, and her eyes drifted closed as she finally began to relax.

"There is no doubt in my mind that you saw a tattoo on the neck of the robber." Connie opened her eyes and met Trace's gaze. "I just want to know *where* on his neck."

"Here." She pointed to the left side of her throat, below her ear and above her shoulder.

"So right here?" Trace asked, placing a feathery kiss on the spot she had just pointed to. "And down a little lower, right?"

Connie gulped, and her pulse climbed as he slowly peppered sweet kisses along the column of her neck. "Oh, yes. That's it. Right there," she breathed and fisted the front of his shirt to keep herself from puddling to the floor.

That was just how good Trace's lips felt on her heated skin. The passion he stirred inside her was quickly growing, and all thoughts of the fashion show, gray eyes and everything else slid to the back of her mind.

This was what she wanted. *Trace* was who she needed.

A low growl that sounded as if it was coming from deep inside his chest reached Connie's ears. She opened her eyes just as he lifted his head.

"I want you so bad, but if this is not what you want, you need to stop me now."

"I want whatever you're willing to give me," she said. "I'm all yours."

"That's all I needed to hear."

Eyes filled with lust, Trace bent slightly, gripped the backs of her thighs and lifted her as if she weighed nothing. Connie wrapped her arms around his neck and her legs around his waist. She loved the feel of him against her as he carried her down the hall toward her bedroom.

Once there, Trace set her on her feet next to the bed and turned on one of the lamps. It cast just enough light to illuminate that part of the room.

"I've been wanting to get you out of this dress all night," he said, his voice thick with need. Connie was glad she wasn't the only one affected by what they were getting ready to do.

He slid the straps off her shoulders, and the dress glided down her body like a feather in the wind and pooled around her feet. She stood before him in nothing but a white thong and high-heeled sandals.

Trace's heated gaze slowly traveled down the length of her partially naked body before working its way back up to her bare breasts. Desire sparked in his eyes, and Connie had to squeeze her legs together to control the throbbing pulse beating at the apex of her thighs.

"You're even more beautiful than I remember." His voice, just above a whisper, was deeper than usual and filled with unadulterated desire. That made her that much more excited. "I can't wait to explore every inch of your sexy body."

He backed her to the bed. Once she was lying down, he took his time undressing. Connie wasn't shy about letting her gaze rake over his muscular body and the tribal tattoo that graced his chest and torso. It was as impressive as the first time she'd seen it on his beautiful dark skin.

The man was a work of art, perfectly sculpted with precise attention to detail. Thick biceps. Check. Six-pack abs. Check. A long, thick shaft that he knew how to use. Check and check. More importantly, tonight he belonged to her.

Connie's eyes followed his every move, even when he tossed a condom onto the nightstand. There were moments in the last few days that she couldn't believe that they were an item. That they were building a relationship that exceeded just having a good friendship.

Trace reached for her foot and planted soft kisses up her leg as he unbuckled her sandal. She squirmed with every touch of his lips to her skin and then started giggling.

"Tra-a-ce. That tickles." She twisted and wiggled, trying to get him to let go of her leg, but he held tight.

Flashing a wicked grin, he proceeded to give her other leg the same treatment. When both shoes were removed, her thong was all that was left. He sprinkled kisses over her stomach and along the waistband of her thong, then slid the silky material down her legs. He dropped it to the floor and climbed onto the bed next to her.

Connie shivered when Trace's cold fingertip touched her chest, and he slowly glided it downward, only stopping when he reached her belly button.

"I'm going to have fun with you tonight, and I'm starting right here." He lowered his head, and when his mouth touched hers, spirals of ecstasy charged through her body.

She wound her arms around Trace's neck and savored the sweet caress of his lips. With every lap of his tongue, the intensity of their lip-lock grew. He kissed her with a passion that rivaled every other kiss between them.

As his tongue explored the interior recesses of her mouth, Trace slid his hand down her body, and her skin tingled everywhere he touched. A moan crawled up Connie's throat when he cupped one of her breasts. Squeezing her gently, he ran the pad of his thumb over her hardened nipple.

She hadn't been with a man since the last time they'd slept together, and she already knew it wasn't going to take much for her to lose control.

"Man, you feel good," he murmured against her lips before he moved his mouth lower. Where his hand was caressing her breast moments ago, his mouth and tongue took over.

Connie squirmed beneath him, her hand on the back of his head as he sucked, teased and pushed her closer to her breaking point. It was when his hand slid between her thighs that she involuntarily squeezed her legs together, trying to prolong the intense pleasure building within. Trace wasn't deterred, though. His finger found its way between her slick folds, and Connie whimpered when he slid inside her.

"Trace," she breathed. Her hips moved in rhythm with each stroke of his finger as he slipped it in and out of her. Her nails dug into his arms as the pressure building inside her intensified. "I can't hold…" Her words were cut off when he slid another digit inside her and increased his speed. An electrical current arced within her, and Connie lost it. She began screaming Trace's name over and over as an orgasm swept through her body and pushed her over the edge of control.

"I love watching you come," he whispered, "and I'm not done with you yet."

Body wound tight, Trace reached over and snatched the condom from the nightstand. Watching her release had him barely holding on to his own control. Even now, her body was still vibrating with aftershocks, and he couldn't wait to get inside her.

He quickly sheathed himself. So much for taking his time with her tonight. He wanted to go slow and get reacquainted with her luscious body, but that wasn't going to happen. At least not with this first round. He wanted her too much.

"You are so damn beautiful," he said, and a satiated smile lifted the corners of her sexy mouth.

Man, this woman. This sweet, gorgeous woman was all his, and he planned to satisfy her every desire. The last time they'd been together, she'd made it clear that they could only be friends. Trace had vowed right then and there that he wasn't giving up. He knew in his heart that she would be his one day, and since things had changed between them, his dream was coming true.

"You've been enticing me with this magnificent body for days—tonight and going forward, you're *mine*."

"I'm totally okay with that," she said saucily, her eyes glittering with mischief.

He hovered above her and nudged her thighs apart before easing into her sweet heat. Damn, she felt good and snug. Her inner muscles tightened around his shaft, and it took everything within Trace to hold on and not lose control.

He kissed her as he started moving inside her, and before long, they rocked in perfect sync, like an intricate melody slowly building to a higher pitch. They hadn't been together in over a month, but their bodies were still flawlessly in tune. With each thrust, Connie rotated her hips, matching him stroke for stroke as he went deeper and harder.

Trace pulled his mouth from hers. "Connie…baby," he said as he drove into her faster. He knew he wouldn't be able to hang on much longer, especially with the way her sex clenched and unclenched around his length. She felt too damn good, and his control was teetering closer to the edge.

"Ahhhh, T-Trace!" Connie screamed after one last powerful thrust. Her body bucked and jerked beneath him as her head brushed back and forth against the pillow. Watching her fall apart again, and the turbulence from her orgasm, pushed him to his own release.

Trace collapsed on top of her, but quickly lifted up on his elbow, not wanting to put all of his weight on her. After catching his breath, he rolled onto his back and pulled her to his side. Their heavy breathing mingled as their panting filled the quietness in the room.

"Damn…that was intense."

Still gasping for air, Connie nodded, her wild curls brushing against his chest. "Yeah…intense."

Once his heart rate was somewhat back to normal, he gave Connie a quick kiss and headed to the bathroom to dispose of the condom. When Trace climbed back into the bed, Connie's eyes were barely open. But she smiled at him, and his heart did a little jig inside his chest.

She was his. He was hers.

Trace wrapped his arm around her, and she snuggled up against him, but he didn't close his eyes. They needed to finish the conversation from earlier.

"Sweetheart?"

"Hmm." Connie sounded as if she might've drifted off. Trace shook her a little, and she propped her chin on his chest. "I'm awake, and if you're going to tell me that you're not done with me yet, I already know."

Trace laughed. "Ah, you know me well, then. I'll never get enough of you, but that's not what I was going to say."

Connie met his gaze. "Okay, what were you going to say?"

"In the kitchen, before you distracted me with your tempting neck, we were discussing me not believing you."

"Trace, I know you believe me. I shouldn't have said otherwise. I guess when you were so quiet in the car, and then you said the guy didn't have a tattoo…" She shrugged. "I started doubting. Not just you, but doubting myself, too. What if I didn't really see what I thought I saw?"

"I believe you saw a tattoo on that man's neck. Me

being silent in the car wasn't about you. It was more about me being disappointed in myself. I was reckless tonight. I should've handled Gray Eyes differently or not at all. That situation in that back room could've gone bad real quick."

"Umm, it actually did," Connie said. "I thought you were going to hurt the guy, and there was a moment I thought he'd hurt you. His eye color is not the only thing unusual about him. There was something unsettling in his stare."

Trace had sensed that also. "Did you feel that way when you ran into him at the restaurant?"

Connie shook her head. "No, but it could be that I missed it because I was shocked to see him. Or at least see his eyes. Remember when I said that I've seen him or those gray eyes before?"

"Yes."

"Well, I'm thinking I must have seen him at the sandwich shop in passing."

Trace nodded. That was possible, especially since the owner had said that the guy had been there a few times.

"Why'd you choose to corner him in that room instead of just calling the cops?" Connie asked and laid her head back on Trace's chest.

"And tell the cops what? The guy hadn't officially done anything. Yes, you recognized that he had the same unusual eye color as the robber, but outside of that, we had nothing. We both know that eye color is not a crime."

"It's not just that that made him stand out. It was

something in his eyes. An emptiness. A coldness. I swear I felt a chill when we made eye contact at the bank."

"Did you feel that tonight with the model?"

After a slight hesitation, Connie said, "Not exactly. Tonight wasn't a coldness that I saw or sensed. It was more like…creepiness."

Trace kissed the top of her head. "Well, hopefully we won't run into him again."

Trace wanted to believe they had, but his gut told him that they hadn't seen the last of John Doe.

# Chapter 18

Trace's eyes eased open, and he blinked several times, slowly adjusting to the semidarkness in the bedroom. Moonlight crept in between the slats of the blinds, allowing just enough light for him to make out portions of the room.

He lay still, wondering what had awakened him. Listening for any sounds, he only heard Connie's soft snores. He glanced down at where she was snuggled against him, her head resting on his chest and her wild curls hiding her face.

Despite how things had turned out at the fashion show, the rest of the evening had been amazing. If there was such a thing as being addicted to a person, that was what he was. He couldn't imagine them going back to status quo: being just friends.

After their first round of sex, they'd gotten up and bumped around in the kitchen in search of snacks. Everything from leftover chicken and vegetables to popcorn and trail mix had made it to their plates. More importantly, they talked about anything and everything, from the latest movies they'd seen to favorite sex positions. No subject was off-limits. Once they were finished eating and chatting, they had tidied up the kitchen and returned to the bedroom for another round of mindblowing sex. That was why he should've been knocked out, like Connie, but Trace had never been a sound sleeper.

He brushed his hand up and down Connie's hip and felt his eyes drift closed as sleep gently pulled him back under. No sooner had he felt himself falling into a deep sleep than he heard his cell phone on the bedside table vibrating.

Trace tensed. Nothing good ever came from a phone call at three o'clock in the morning.

Trying not to wake Connie, he stretched out his left arm and twisted slightly until his hand made contact with the device. Squinting, he glanced at the screen and saw his brother's name.

Langston.

"Yeah," he answered.

"I have it on good authority that there was a breach with the bank's security footage that the FBI obtained," Langston said by way of greeting. "They were able to tell that someone else was viewing the video of the robbery while the Feds were viewing it."

The unease from a moment ago quickly exploded

into foreboding. Trace didn't have to ask what bank, but *why* bounced around inside his head.

"Not sure who or why," Langston continued, as if reading Trace's mind. "The tech team assumes the hacker was looking for something. Or someone. I'm letting you know because I took a look at the footage, Trace. There's a good shot of Connie."

Trace bolted upright, forgetting that Connie was lying on him. She mumbled something in her sleep and turned onto her side, her back facing him.

"When did all of this happen?" he questioned, his voice low. "I mean, how long have the Feds known there might've been a breach?"

"I'm thinking they got the video the day of the robbery, but I have no idea when they realized the problem." Langston had been whispering during the whole conversation. Now there was an echo in the background, as if he was walking through a tunnel. "I found out a few hours ago, but just had a chance to give you a heads-up."

"Where are you?"

"Out and about," he said.

Trace assumed his brother was on some type of assignment. Otherwise, he would've called earlier and not in the middle of the night.

"I'm heading home in a few, and before you ask, I don't have anything else to share. This all might be a whole lot of nothing. It can even be a glitch in the system, but the tech team definitely believes someone hacked that part of the bank's network. By the way, you didn't hear this from me. They're trying to keep it quiet until they know…"

The crashing sounds of glass breaking and a loud thunk snatched Trace's attention. "Stay on the line," he whispered and hastily slipped on his pants, then grabbed his gun.

Hurrying to the bedroom door, he cracked it open and glanced down the short hallway.

His heart slammed against his chest, and shock lodged in his gut.

*Flames.*

Before he could form a thought, the smoke detector blared.

"Trace!" his brother yelled in his ear, panic in his voice. "What is that? What's happening?"

Trace hurried and closed the door. *"Fire."* He quickly rattled off Connie's address into the phone and learned that his brother was nearby. "Head this way, but don't come to the house. We're going to need a ride. I'll call with our location."

Connie jerked awake and bolted upright in bed, her bare breasts on full display and her hair sticking up all over. "What's going—?"

"Get up," Trace said in a rush. "We gotta get out of here."

His heart pounded double time as his mind raced. His thoughts were all over the place as he stuck his gun in the back of his waistband and dropped his cell phone into his pants pocket. Then he snatched his dress shirt from a nearby chair and shrugged into it. Trace didn't bother buttoning it while he slid his bare feet into his dress shoes. After grabbing his wallet and keys from the nightstand, he shoved them into his other pocket, then glanced around to see if he needed anything else.

There was just enough illumination from the attached bathroom's night-light to cast a shadow around Connie. She stood in a daze as if still not comprehending that they needed to leave.

"Sweetheart, get dressed," Trace said in a hurry. He bent down and snatched up his discarded T-shirt from the night before and tossed it to her.

She finally started moving, and he dashed to the bedroom door again and touched it. *Hot.* Carefully, he also touched the doorknob, which was hotter. That was when he noticed the smoke seeping in beneath the door.

"*Damn.* Sweetheart, we gotta get out of here."

He yanked the covers from the bed and pushed them against the bottom of the door, then headed to the window overlooking the backyard. There was a short drop to the ground. He'd have no problem making it, but it might be a bit much for Connie.

"Trace?"

"Grab your purse. We have to go out this way." Nothing else might be salvageable.

"But…"

Trace opened the window, punched out the screen and stuck his head out. This was one of those times when he was glad the light on Connie's garage wasn't on. Seeing no one, he pulled his head back into the room. The sleepiness on Connie's face seconds ago—gone. Now there was fear.

At least she had put on the T-shirt. It also looked like

she might've slipped on a pair of shorts. He had no idea what was in the backpack that she held, but he was glad she was finally moving.

"I'm going to jump first, and I need you to be right behind me, all right?"

Trace hated the idea of leaving her in the house, even for a second. But if they were going to get out of there in one piece, he had to go first.

"But—"

"This is the only way out," he said before she could ask anything. "We gotta move. *Now.*"

"Okay. Okay," she said, rocking from side to side and wringing her hands.

"Don't wait. Follow me out immediately," he demanded.

When Trace started climbing out of the window and glanced back at her, she was still looking around the room.

"*Now*, Connie."

Trace put his legs through the window opening before sliding the rest of his body out. Gripping the sill, he dangled for a second, then dropped to the ground with a soft touch. He glanced up. Connie tossed the backpack and he caught it and quickly put it on.

Then Trace saw that she was out the window and hanging on the sill.

"Come on, sweetie," he whispered loud enough for only her to hear. "Just drop. I got you."

Connie did as he said and fell into his arms. She was such a lightweight. He didn't bother lowering her to the ground, especially since she had on flip-flops.

Trace carried her, ignoring her whispered protests to be put down. She changed tactics, questioning him about where they were going, but he still didn't respond. He positioned her in a fireman's carry over his shoulder. Once he had a good hold of her, he took off in a run across her graveled backyard. No way was he going to the front of the house; whoever had started the fire would be watching.

Trace cut through the yard of the neighbor directly across from hers, glad there was no fence. Connie's grip on the back of his shirt tightened as he ran through yards, between houses and down sidewalks, trying to stay in the shadows.

He heard a dog's barking from nearby and sirens blared in the distance as Trace picked up speed.

"Trace, stop. Put me down," Connie insisted, her voice raspy and her breaths coming in short spurts, as if she'd been the one running.

"Not yet."

It had to be uncomfortable for her, the way he was bumping her around, but it couldn't be helped. He glanced back over his shoulder to make sure no one was following them. There was no way she'd be able to keep up in flip-flops. Besides, they needed to get at least another block or two from the house.

At that time of the morning, the streets were quiet and the houses were dark. That was working in their favor, at least until they got closer to a main street in the neighborhood. Needing to stay in the shadows, Trace stuck with the side streets and headed for a low-rise apartment complex that was nearby. Connie was quiet, but her grip on the back of his shirt had tightened.

His breaths were coming hard and fast as adrenaline coursed through his veins. A little farther and then he could stop.

Trace had never been so glad to find yards that didn't have fences. When they were a few blocks from her house, he stopped near a tall stucco building, pulled his phone from his pocket and called his brother.

"Where are you?" Langston's voice boomed through the phone, and Trace gave him their location.

"I'm two minutes away, but stay on the line."

"Okay."

Connie shivered next to him, and Trace didn't miss the way she kept swiping at her eyes. His heart ached for her. She'd been through enough the last week to last a lifetime…and now this.

What he saw the first time he'd looked back had propelled him to keep moving. Smoke billowed above Connie's home. Yellow-and-orange flames poured from the windows and kissed the sky. He prayed the fire didn't touch another home, but at the moment, his number one goal was to keep Connie safe.

Trace wrapped his arm around her and held her close. "It's going to be okay," he said. But how could he promise something like that to a person who had just lost everything?

*Almost* everything.

She was alive. *They* were alive.

When he heard her crying, Trace kissed the top of her head, but her sobs came harder. "Aww, baby. I'm so sorry." He didn't know how, and he didn't know when, but he was going to fix this. He was going to find whoever had done this and make them pay.

"Trace? You there?" Langston said into his ear.

"Yeah. Where are you?"

"I'm pulling up. You should see me in a sec."

A large dark SUV with even darker windows slowed in front of the building they were standing at the side of. Trace didn't move until it came to a complete stop. Then he disconnected the call.

"Let's go," he said to Connie.

His arm was wrapped around her as he eased them from against the building. Trace glanced to his left, then right, before hurrying her toward the vehicle. After opening the back door, he ushered her in, then climbed in next to her.

"Thanks for the lift," Trace said. "Do you have a blanket in here?"

"Reach behind you. There should be one in that tray."

Seconds later, Trace wrapped it around Connie, who was trembling to the point of her teeth chattering.

"Is that better?" he asked.

She didn't speak, only nodded.

"Where to?" Langston asked.

Trace hated to do this to Connie, but it needed to be done. "Drive around to her block. I want to see if anyone is outside who looks out of place."

"I don't think I can stand to see the house right now," Connie sobbed, the sound gutting Trace. "And what if they, whoever did this, see us?"

"They won't be able to see inside the vehicle, and Langston won't actually drive down your block."

He probably wouldn't be able to, anyway, since there were likely a couple of fire trucks in front of the house.

She sighed and didn't say anything else, only laid her head against his chest. Trace took that as her giving in to his request.

He glanced at Langston. "Go."

There was nothing like the feeling of emptiness buried deep inside your soul knowing that you had just lost your home. Connie couldn't stop the gut-wrenching, heart-hurting, throat-clogging tears that leaked from her eyes, pulling her into a despair that she knew she'd never rebound from.

As they sat at the street corner, inside Langston's SUV, she watched in horror while yellow-orange flames shot from the roof and seemed to pour from every window of her home. Thick billows of smoke hovered in the sky like an angry thundercloud, looming above all the madness below. It didn't matter that tons of firefighters were hosing down the house, trying hard to put out the fire. All she saw was her hard work—her world—going up in flames.

Her head hurt. Her heart ached.

How had this craziness of the past week become her life?

One day she was on top of the world with a great job, wonderful friends and a beautiful home. Then, within a heartbeat, everything changed. Bank robbery. Murders. Hit-and-run.

Now this.

The faster Connie wiped her eyes, the faster tears fell. The horrid stench of burning wood, tar, metal and wires… It was too much. It was all too much. A chilling numbness seeped into her bones and hung out there like an unwanted guest.

Connie dropped back against Trace, defeat weighing heavy in her chest. Sitting in the back seat of Langston's SUV with Trace's arms firmly wrapped around her helped. Yes, she was alive. Yes, she was safe. But right now, it still didn't feel like it was enough.

She closed her eyes, trying to block out the sight of literally seeing her entire life go up in smoke. What if Trace hadn't been there? What if he hadn't moved into action immediately? When she woke up to the blaring of her smoke detector, her mind was full of fog. It had taken several minutes for her to wrap her brain around what was going on.

Again, the what-ifs started clogging her mind. Seemed she'd been pondering what-ifs a lot lately.

"Trace, where's your car?" Langston asked.

"In the shop."

Connie hadn't even thought about her own car, parked in the garage. From where Langston had stopped his truck, at the corner of the block, the back of her house was out of view. She didn't know if the fire had reached the garage. At the moment, Connie couldn't think about that. She just kept her eyes closed, hoping to draw in some type of comfort in knowing that she and Trace were safe. They were alive.

*That should be enough*, she thought.

"Do you see anyone who looks out of place?" Langston asked. "Does anyone stand out? Some arsonists like to stick around and see their handiwork."

Connie wasn't sure if he was talking to her or Trace. Neither of them said a word, but if she knew Trace, he was probably looking at everybody and everything. Cataloging every detail of the scene.

As for her? She kept her eyes closed, unable to watch any longer. She had seen enough.

The silence in the car grew. Trace said nothing for a few minutes. Only held her tight enough to almost cause damage to her ribs. Connie opened her eyes and glanced at him. He was staring at something. She followed his line of view to a spot across the street from her house. Some of her neighbors, the ones who lived on each side of her, were outside, huddled together. There were also other people that she couldn't identify.

"What is it, Trace?" she asked.

"It might not be anything, but there's a guy in a black sweatshirt standing to the side by himself. He's close enough to the small crowd to blend in, but also far enough away not to be noticed."

Trace pulled out his phone. Connie wasn't sure who he was calling that time of night… No, actually, it was morning. Either way, it was too early to be calling people. But instead of calling someone, he shot off a quick text.

"We can leave," he told Langston. "Since you don't live too far from here, take us home with you until I figure out next steps."

"No problem" was all Langston said before he started driving.

"Who did you text?" Connie asked.

"Indie. It's too late to reach the fashion-show organizers tonight, and I don't want to wait for morning. I'm hoping she can help because I need to know the real name of the gray-eyed man. Because it sure as hell ain't John Doe."

# *Chapter 19*

Thirty minutes later, Langston turned into a new development that included single-family homes and town houses. Mixed feelings gripped Connie. She had just gone house hunting with her sister recently; who'd have thought she'd soon need to do the same for herself? Riding through the neighborhood also made her think about Richard. All of this craziness in her life started at the bank and with him, her loan officer.

*Don't think. Just try to relax*, Connie told herself. She'd drive herself nuts if she kept replaying everything in her mind.

After a few more turns through the neighborhood, Langston pulled into the driveway of a home a little bigger than hers. The overhead door of the two-car attached garage lifted, and he drove in and parked. It had been a quiet ride to his place, and even now, no one spoke. Connie was thankful for that. After leaving her home, she wasn't really in the mood to talk, though she would have to at some point.

Once the overhead door went back down, Langston left them in the SUV and went into the house.

Trace didn't move. His head was back against the seat, and he stared straight ahead. If he was like her, he was probably emotionally and mentally exhausted. But what if something else was wrong?

"Trace," she said, concern bubbling inside her. He didn't respond, but he'd heard her. He rubbed his hand up and down her arm slowly, seeming to be in no hurry to move.

Connie released a long, exhausted breath and laid her head back on his chest. The steady beat of his heart was almost soothing, or at least it would be if she could stop thinking. If she could stop thinking about how afraid she'd been when she dropped out of the bedroom window, maybe she could relax.

Despite the warm temperature in the car, a cold chill scurried down her spine. Memories of waking up to a burning house formed in her mind. No one should be awakened from a deep sleep like that, disoriented and scared.

Then there was Trace. Connie hadn't missed the worry in his eyes right before he went out the window. Had he honestly thought she wouldn't follow him? Little did he know, she would follow him to the moon if necessary.

She trusted him.

Trusted him more than she had ever trusted another man.

"Thank you for saving my life tonight," she said in the quietness of the SUV.

He placed a kiss on top of her head. "There's nothing in the world I wouldn't do for you."

"What made you decide to leave the house once we were outside? Why didn't we wait for the fire department?"

"When I'm on protection duty, I try to think of worst-case scenarios and plan from there. Not that I had planned for what we just went through." He shook his head. "That—that caught me totally off guard. On some of our assignments, especially the ones involving abusive spouses or stalkers, I try to think like the would-be attacker."

"I don't understand."

Connie admired all of their security specialists, and she was sure she didn't know half the craziness they had to deal with on assignments. Sure, there were debriefings, especially after certain assignments. Yet she wouldn't be surprised to learn that their team probably kept some things to themselves.

"For instance, the fire tonight was started by somebody. If I set a house on fire intentionally, I'd want to see if the people got out. I'd want to know if the coroners had to be called in.

"So with those thoughts, I formed a plan. I didn't see anyone in the backyard. So, at least for a little while, whoever set the fire will think that you're still in there. Or that we're still in there."

"Dear God. How do people live with themselves when they do stuff like that? I just…I just can't wrap my brain around that. Now there's a chance that my neighbors will think I'm dead. That I burned up in the fire."

"Maybe. Or they'll think you weren't home, especially if they don't know your car is in the garage. We're going to need to contact the Feds on the bank-robbery case, or I'll get Langston to do it. Either way, they need to know what's going on, since I'm ninety-nine percent sure that fire is connected to the robbers. But there's also a chance that it could be connected to the grayeyed dude. I was hoping to hear from Indie by now."

"Trace, it hasn't been that long since you texted her, and it's also early in the morning."

"I know." He shrugged. "Hopefully, she knows that guy's name and can give me some information on him. I don't want her involved in this mess. So if I can get that information without having the Feds contact her, it'll be better."

"Okay." Connie yawned noisily before she could cover it up. "Sorry."

"No need to be sorry. Let's get you inside."

"Trace, if it was the bank robbers who set the fire, that means they know who I am."

He released a long sigh and brushed some of her hair away from her face. "Yeah, I know."

"How is that possible? I just don't understand any of this. Why me? Why come after me? Do they know that I can partially ID one of them?"

She rattled off one question after another, getting

angrier by the minute. Why was any of this happening to her, and when would it be over?

Trace told her about the call he'd gotten from Langston right before the fire. Neither of them knew enough to make any assumptions, but Trace promised to get answers.

Connie rubbed her temples, feeling overwhelmed with what little they did know. "Assuming that this fire is attached to the robbers or the guy at the fashion show, I want to know how they got my information."

"Yeah, that's what I'm planning to find out."

After getting Connie settled into his brother's guest room, Trace headed downstairs to the main level. When he strolled into the kitchen, Langston was sitting on one of the bar stools, typing on his laptop.

"Do you have anything stronger than beer in this place?" Trace asked as he perused the inside of the refrigerator.

"There's rum in the cabinet over the coffee maker."

Trace found the half-empty bottle and grabbed a glass. Instead of pouring two fingers' worth, he doubled the amount.

"Rough night, huh?" Langston said without looking up from his computer screen.

Trace gulped half the glass of liquor, slammed his eyes shut and winced at the burn going down his throat. "You could say that," he croaked. "Damn, this stuff is strong."

"That's the good stuff. Better to sip it than to slam it back."

"Now you tell me."

Trace dropped into one of the chairs at the small glass table and held his head. He was dog-tired, but he needed answers before he could get any sleep.

"I thought you said you were going to ride the bachelor train until the rails wear out."

Trace glanced at his brother. Yeah, he remembered that conversation a few years ago when Langston was having woman problems. They had both agreed that the single life was the best life.

"What makes you think that's not still the case?" Trace asked and took another sip of the dark liquor. It burned like hell going down his throat.

"Any blind person could see that you're in love with Connie. I've never seen you look all googly-eyed at anyone. At least not the way you were doing earlier."

Trace chuckled. "Googly-eyed. Seriously?"

When he and Connie had entered the house, Trace formally introduced her to Langston, even though they'd met briefly a few months ago at the office.

"I don't do googly eyes," Trace responded weakly. He was crazy about Connie, but was surprised his brother could tell just from the brief interaction. "Besides, she just went through a traumatic experience. I'm worried about her and want to make sure she's all right."

Langston shook his head. "Nah, bro. Tell it to someone who doesn't know you. You're in love with that woman." He lifted his hand when Trace started to speak. "Save it. You don't have to defend or deny it. I was just making an observation. Nothing you can say will make me think otherwise. Besides, there's nothing wrong with you being in love. I like her."

"You don't even know her."

His brother's opinion of Connie meant a lot, he admitted to himself, and Trace looked forward to introducing her to the rest of the family. When he did, it would be the first—and only, if he had his way—time that he would introduce them to a woman he was serious about.

"I might not know her well, but I saw how she handled herself tonight. She's a tough woman. I also noticed the same sickening you're-my-everything expression in her eyes when she looked at you." He shivered dramatically and made an expression of mock disgust. "I'm not sure what she sees in you, but she gawked at you like you hung the moon or something."

A slow grin spread across Trace's mouth. "Don't hate, man. It ain't a good look on you."

Langston laughed and grabbed the bottle of rum. He poured two fingers' worth and sat in the chair across from Trace.

"Tell me about her," he said, shocking the heck out of Trace. "I know she's the VP of Operations at LEPA, but what else do you know about her?"

Out of all his siblings, he and Langston were the closest. Not just because they were less than two years apart, but because they used to do everything together. But Trace could count on one hand how many times they'd discussed women they were interested in.

"She's…amazing. Tough, yet gentle. Hardworking. But knows how to have fun. Sweet. But don't take crap from nobody. Independent…well, she's independent and stubborn as hell."

They both laughed.

For the next few minutes, Trace told him about his and Connie's relationship without sharing too much. The more Trace talked about her, the more he felt his heart swell with love. He wasn't sure exactly when his feelings for her had grown more intense, but he couldn't imagine not having her in his life now.

"I don't know, man." Trace took a sip of his drink, struggling to explain how this pint-size woman had snagged his heart. "I just… I like the way she makes me feel. Like I'm invincible, powerful, and like she needs me even though she's self-sufficient. She also listens, even if I'm not really saying anything. If that makes any sense."

Langston nodded as if he knew exactly what Trace was talking about. His brother had only been in one serious relationship that Trace could remember. When it ended, Langston had changed, gotten harder and more guarded. He dated on occasion, but never anything serious.

"I'm also comfortable with her. It's like we've known each other forever. Like she's always been a part of me." Trace shrugged, unable to explain it any better than that.

"I get it." Langston took another sip of his drink. "I'm heading to bed soon. Oh, and I forgot to tell you that I shot Max a quick text while we were outside of Connie's house."

"He knows about the fire?"

Langston nodded. "I told him that you think it's arson

and might be connected to the bank robbers. Like you, he thinks it's a good idea for Connie to lie low."

"Once we figure out who the man is, Connie can give the info to the Feds who are overseeing the bank-robbery case. Actually, you can relay the info," Trace said.

"Nah, let Connie or Max do it."

"Why can't you contact them? I assume they're working out of the same office as you."

Langston didn't say anything for a few seconds as he slowly slid his finger down the side of his glass. "Agents don't like when other agents get involved in their cases. Since I know Connie, they might see it as me trying to take over."

"That's crazy. You guys are a team." Trace thought about those he'd served with while in the navy. He had no doubt if he needed any of them, for anything, all it would take was a phone call. They all understood the importance of being there for each other.

"Some Federal agents see each other as team members. Others? Not so much. Their main goal is getting to the top by any means. They aren't trying to be friends. Nor do they want to take the chance that another agent will make them look bad. Those individuals see other agents as competition."

Trace had a feeling there was a story there, but knew his brother probably wouldn't share it.

"Is that why you've been thinking more about us moving the timeline up on starting our private investigation business?"

He and Langston had been discussing going into business together for years. Since they were problem solvers by nature and enjoyed helping people, PI work would be a natural fit.

"Yeah, partly. Mainly, I'm ready for a career change, and I'm looking forward to us building something of our own. I was thinking that we should talk to Trinity. There might be a way for us to do some type of partnership, since both businesses would complement the other."

"I think that's a great idea. Knowing her, she'd be all for some type of collaboration."

Langston slammed back the rest of his drink. "It's four thirty in the morning. I need to get some sleep, but what's next as it relates to Connie and the fire? You sounded positive that the model had something to do with it."

"I don't know for sure. It's just a gut feeling. That reminds me." Trace dug into the front pocket of his tuxedo pants and pulled out his cell phone. "Can I use the computer in your office? I want to watch the restaurant video again. I'll be able to see it better on a bigger device."

"Go ahead."

They headed down the hall to Langston's home office that played double duty as an art studio. Growing up, he could always be found sketching or doing paintings. Now he was as good as a professional artist. Trace didn't know why his brother didn't want to sell any of his work.

After Langston logged in to the computer, he moved and let Trace sit at the desk. Minutes later, Trace had pulled up the copy of the video that Nancy had given him.

"What are we looking for?" Langston asked as he watched the video from over Trace's shoulder.

"I'm not sure yet, but days after we were at the restaurant, Connie realized her wallet was missing. I have a hunch."

They watched the video footage, and the second time through it, Trace stopped it midway.

"Did you see that?" he asked his brother and pointed at the gray-eyed man. "Her purse strap is sliding down her shoulder and the bag itself is kind of sitting on the floor next to her."

"Looks like dude actually bumped into her. He's close enough to reach inside her bag." Langston tapped Trace's shoulder. "Move and let me try something."

Trace switched places with him and watched as his brother opened another program on the computer.

"I might be able to reduce the video speed." Langston typed in a couple of commands. Within minutes, they were watching the footage in slow motion.

A few minutes in, Trace had his answer. "Son of… I guess we know what happened to her wallet." The guy was smooth in slipping his hand in and out of her purse. If Langston hadn't slowed down the video, they would've missed it again. "That means he could've easily gotten her address from her driver's license."

Langston nodded. "Now all you need is his name."

"Yeah, that's where Indie comes in at. I texted her, but haven't heard back yet. If I don't hear from her soon, then I'll contact the fashion-show organizers to see what they know about our mystery man. Once I have his name, then I'll forward it to Maxwell. Not sure if he can do much, but the cops can take him in for questioning regarding the fire, if nothing else."

"True, and be sure to send the info to the agents on the robbery case," Langston added.

"I will."

Langston stretched his arms out and yawned. "All right, man. If there's nothing else, I'm calling it a—"

"Wait. Before you shut your computer down, do you have access to a database that contains pictures of prison and gang tattoos? Max gave me a copy of the sketch that Connie helped with." Trace dug the piece of paper out of his wallet.

"You don't think the agents on the case already looked through the catalog for a match?" Langston asked as he opened the software.

"I don't know, but I'd feel better if I went through it myself. Actually, I'm thinking maybe you and I both should look through it. This'll be good practice for when we start our PI business."

"I guess, but I'm going to need coffee. Lots of coffee. Want some?"

"Sure."

Two hours later, the sun was peeking through the blinds, signaling that it was officially morning. They were still camped out in the office, and Trace was glad they'd finally made progress.

"It's safe to say it's a gang tattoo."

Trace was impressed that Connie had been able to give enough details to the sketch artist. The partial drawing wasn't exact, but the little they had was close enough for them to tell that it could be a match.

"More specifically, it's the One-Seven Crew tattoo. They're one of the most dangerous gangs on the West

Coast. They mostly reside in Los Angeles, and as far as I know, there's been no activity here in town."

"Maybe they're moving into Vegas territory," Trace reasoned.

"Maybe, and the sketch of the tat is slightly different than this one." Langston pointed at the colorful photo of the tattoo on the computer screen. "See this part of the tattoo, where the capital $N$ is dangling from the right side of the triangle?"

"Yeah."

"Well, it's the symbol for a neophyte, a gang member still needing to prove himself. The string of bank robberies might be part of the initiation process. The guy's tat is probably not even completed yet."

Trace shook his head. "You trying to tell me that this crew would let him get a tattoo before he's even all the way in?"

Langston shrugged and sat back in his seat. "Crazier things than that happen in gangs, man."

It felt like Trace's head was going to explode. Partly because he was exhausted. The other reason was because he feared Connie was now on a gang member's radar.

"You know, I'm thinking…" Langston said as he swiveled back and forth in his desk chair. "If the bank robberies are a part of some initiation, the One-Seven Crew aren't going to want any trouble. If one of these neophytes gets caught in the process, the gang bosses might claim no affiliation."

"Yeah, and…?" Trace wasn't sure where Langston was going with his thought process.

"And that might be why the bank teller was killed. Those who robbed the bank are probably lying low since authorities know the teller helped them. Now that she's dead, that's one loose string tied up."

A sense of foreboding lodged inside Trace's chest. "You're saying that Connie might be a loose end?"

"Maybe, but I'd bet my paycheck that no one in the One-Seven knows Connie exists, except the guy she made eye contact with. This man is probably taking heat for getting the bank teller involved in the first place, which was why he had to off her.

"He's not going to want his crew to know that some other woman at the bank might've saw his tat. Because if his crew found out, they'd kill his ass before authorities could get a hold of him."

"So for this neophyte, Connie is a loose end," Trace said again, more to himself than to his brother. "Even if he doesn't know whether or not she can ID him. He can't take that risk."

Langston was tapping his fingers on the desktop. "True, but why was he modeling? Assuming it's the same guy."

Trace's head was spinning. He didn't know enough about gangs, organized crime or any of that. All he knew was that his woman was in danger.

"Damn, this is messed up," he said and started pacing the floor in front of the desk, trying to process all that he had learned so far.

Langston brought up a good point, though. If the guy thought Connie or anyone might've seen his tat or could identify him in any way, why was he modeling? Nothing was making sense.

*Unless the bank robbery has nothing to do with the gray-eyed model.*

There were plenty of gray-eyed people in the world. Granted, that guy's were the most unusual shade of gray that Trace had ever seen. Still…

"Something that still has me stumped is that the model didn't have a tattoo," Trace said. "I'm thinking he might just be some chump who had seen Connie at the restaurant before and wanted to get close to her. He didn't have a tat, so—"

"You might not have seen the tat. That doesn't mean he didn't have one," Langston countered. "There's all types of makeup or other methods that models and actors use to change their appearance. Hell, for all we know, the gray eyes could be contacts."

"Aw, hell." Trace gripped his head and growled as frustration charged through his body. That was not what he wanted to hear. If this guy set Connie's house on fire and went around camouflaging his looks, they were screwed.

Trace's cell phone vibrated on the desk, and he reached over and grabbed it. Glancing at the screen, he saw that it was a text from Indie.

His name is Daniel Atkinson.

# *Chapter 20*

Connie leaned her back against the headboard and took a careful sip of the steaming hot coffee that she had prepared. Her gaze drifted to where Trace was sleeping beside her. He was lying on his stomach with his face buried in the pillow, and his thick arms were wrapped around it tightly. She had no idea how he could sleep like that, let alone breathe.

She wasn't sure when he had gotten into bed, but she had awakened around six and he hadn't been in the room. It was now eight. He couldn't have been asleep long.

Holding the large mug of coffee between both hands, she took another careful sip and glanced around the room. It was large for a guest bedroom. Even with the king-size bed, there was plenty of space for two large nightstands, a dresser and a large comfortable-looking chair near the walk-in closet.

The only problem with the lovely room was that it reminded her of why she was there in the first place. She still couldn't wrap her brain around her circumstances. Technically, she was homeless because some jerk thought it would be a good idea to burn her house down—with her inside it.

A cold chill slithered through her veins. Just thinking about how she could've died last night, and for what? Connie wasn't even sure. That made her angry and sad at the same time. She wished she could blink or tap her heels together a few times and make her life go back to what it was before the bank robbery.

*If only.*

She set the mug on the nightstand and glanced at Trace. Maybe she didn't want everything to go back to the way it was. If it did, that would mean that the two of them would still be *just friends*. Connie never wanted to return to that. It was because of him that she had even survived the last week.

She brought her knees up to her chest and closed her eyes. If only she could stop thinking. She couldn't. Flashbacks came to her in a rush and tears leaked from her eyes. The horror of seeing her house burning would stay with her forever. That emptiness that she felt while sitting inside Langston's car was back.

*What am I going to do?*

*Where do I even begin?*

She covered her face with her hands as an overwhelming wave of sadness engulfed her. This was all too much. Her whole life was falling apart and she didn't know how to fix it. Despair settled around her and seeped into her soul as her sobs came harder and grew louder despite trying to muffle the sound.

*What am I supposed to do?* The question played around and around inside her mind. For the most part, she'd had an easy life and could handle just about everything. But this? This was too much.

Connie didn't know how long she sat there crying when she felt a hand on her bare leg.

"Sweetie, we're going to get through this."

Trace's sleep-filled voice penetrated through her thoughts, and Connie frantically wiped her face before looking at him. He had already seen her at her worst, but she didn't want him to see her still crying.

He was staring at her with bloodshot eyes, and he looked absolutely exhausted. That almost made her start crying all over again. She knew he'd stayed up to get answers…for her. Considering the crap he'd been going through with her this past week, it was a wonder he hadn't run for the hills.

His large hand was still on her leg and he squeezed. "I promise things are going to get better. Don't lose hope, okay?"

Not trusting herself to speak, all Connie could do was nod. When Trace turned onto his back and opened his arm to her, she didn't waste any time snuggling against him. Her head on his chest with his arms wrapped tightly around her helped ease some of the melancholy that had settled inside her.

She inhaled deeply, soaked up his fresh scent, then slowly released the breath.

"Thank you...for everything you've done for me and all that you're doing," she said. "I can't imagine going through these last few days with anyone but you."

"You don't have to thank me." His deep, raspy voice sounded so tired, but that didn't stop him from trying to comfort her. "There's no other place I'd rather be than right here with you. Except maybe on a beach somewhere, but definitely with you."

"A beach sounds wonderful right now." Connie closed her eyes and tried to imagine huge waves crashing against rocks and seagulls shrieking in the distance. She and Trace would be lounging on the white sandy beach as if they didn't have a care in the world.

"I still owe you a real first date. How about when this is all over, we take some time off and go to the Bahamas?"

Connie opened her eyes and glanced at him. "Really? Will I get to meet your dad?"

Trace gave her a tired smile and nodded. "Yeah. We'll stay in a hotel, though, because you get a little loud when we make love."

Connie's mouth dropped open. "*Me?* I wasn't the only one screaming my release, if I remember correctly."

"Men don't scream. *I* don't scream. What you heard was a growl or a roar. Definitely not a scream."

"All right, if you say so, but I'm pretty sure you were screaming 'uncle.'"

He chuckled, and Connie returned her head to his chest, enjoying the way his hand glided up and down her hip. And just like that, he managed to pull her out of her funk. Her heart might be aching for the home she had lost, but being with Trace reminded her of what was most important in life. Family and friends.

Acknowledging that made her think about her parents. It was time she put the past in the past and reconnected with both of them. Just because she didn't agree with a lot of their decisions when she was growing up didn't mean that she didn't still love them.

That was her last thought before drifting back to sleep.

A few hours later, Connie climbed the stairs with a tray of food. When she came up with the idea of giving Trace brunch in bed, she hadn't realized what a pain it would be carrying food to the second floor.

When she reached the top landing, Trace was exiting the hallway bathroom with a towel around his neck and clothes in his hand.

"I'm so glad you're awake. Can you help me?" Connie asked. He'd been asleep when she'd gone downstairs to cook, but, boy, was she glad he was awake. Her arms were like limp noodles from carrying the heavy tray.

Trace hurried toward her and reached for the tray with his free hand. "What's all of this?"

"Whew, thanks. That was tiring," Connie said and shook out her arms. "I wanted to do something special for you. Before Langston left the house, he told me to make myself at home. So I made you breakfast. Well, actually, brunch."

"That's sweet of you, but this tray was too heavy

for you to be carrying up the stairs. I could've eaten in the kitchen."

"Then it wouldn't be breakfast in bed. Now come on and get back in bed."

Trace chuckled. "I'm right behind you."

He followed her into the bedroom and dropped his clothes into a nearby chair. Connie repositioned the pillows on the bed, then took the tray from him.

"Now get in."

"Boy, you're bossy this morning." He did as he was told and climbed onto the bed before taking the tray from her. Connie settled in next to him.

"Can't say that I've ever had breakfast in bed."

Connie's eyebrows shot up. "Really?" He shook his head while chewing a piece of bacon. "That's great. That means you're having a *first* with me."

"Sweetheart, I plan to have a lot of firsts with you." With a finger under her chin, he pulled her close, then kissed her lips. "Feel free to give me breakfast in bed anytime."

"I'll keep that in mind."

He pointed at the three plates that were on the tray. "I assume this is for both of us?"

"I ate a little while I was downstairs." She actually didn't have much of an appetite, which wasn't unusual. That was usually the first thing to go when she was worried or stressed about something.

"How'd you sleep?" Trace asked, digging into the hash browns as if he hadn't eaten in weeks.

"Okay. Kept waking up, but thanks to you, I was able to sleep soundly for a few hours. You must be exhausted. I actually thought you'd still be at least lying down."

"I'm all right. I took a quick shower and that helped. I knew we needed to start planning our next steps."

"Does that mean you know who set the fire?"

"Not yet."

Connie had already contacted the insurance company, but it would take a few days before the insurance adjusters could get to the house and assess the damage.

"Max said the house is unlivable and it doesn't look like anything is salvageable," Connie said.

The whole situation felt so surreal. She'd had a couple of moments throughout the morning where she was trying to make sense of everything. It was still hard to believe that the home that she had saved up to buy was gone.

"When did you talk to him?"

She reached for one of the coffee mugs on the tray. "While I was cooking breakfast. I texted him earlier and asked if he could go by and check out the damage."

Connie had always wanted a big brother, and from the time she and Trinity had become roommates in college, Maxwell treated her like a little sister. He even made it his duty to scare off boyfriends that he didn't like. As usual, he came through for her by going by the house.

"What else did Max say?"

"He said the garage is fine, but I won't be able to pull the car out because of the debrief in the driveway. He put caution tape around the property and is supposed to check and see if maybe he can clear out the driveway. Then he'll move my car to someplace safe."

Connie had also talked to Trinity and Erica. Both were freaked out, but grateful that she and Trace were safe.

"I heard from Indie this morning," Trace said. "Our mystery man's name is Daniel Atkinson. He's new on the modeling scene. Indie had never seen or heard of him until the night of the fashion show. I guess the designer recently discovered him."

"Is it possible that he was the guy from the bank?"

Trace gave a slight shrug. "Now, that I don't know. Langston brought up a good point that just because we didn't see a tattoo on this guy doesn't mean he doesn't have one."

"What do you mean?"

"I mean he could've had makeup or something covering that area on his neck."

Connie nodded slowly. She hadn't thought of that. "It would've had to be some pretty heavy-duty stuff. You were really close to him and didn't see signs of a tattoo."

"True, but right now, we're not ruling anything out."

"What did Indie think of the guy? Does she know if he has a tattoo? Did she say he was creepy?"

Trace's eyebrows were scrunched when he glanced at her. "No, she didn't say he was creepy. As a matter of fact, she said he was a really nice guy. The event organizer is planning to use him in other shows."

"So he's probably not the bank robber," Connie said with resignation. She couldn't wait until she could go back to a normal life and not think about robberies or models.

"Maybe not, but he's the one who stole your wallet."

Her head jerked around to Trace so fast, it was a wonder she didn't have whiplash. "What? How do you know?"

He told her how he and Langston had watched the restaurant video again. Connie hadn't even considered that she might've lost her wallet while at the restaurant. The more she learned about this guy, the less she liked.

"Besides credit cards and licenses, what else was in your wallet?"

Connie sipped her coffee and tried to recall what she'd had in the wallet. It wasn't much. "I had a few dollars in there and maybe a few business cards, including my own."

"Okay, so he knows where you work. We'll need to mention that to Trinity so that she can have some extra guys hang out there until this is over."

"I can take care of that," Connie said, making a mental note of whom to assign and what all they'd need to do to bump up security. "I also had an emergency contact card in my wallet. It has Erica's information on it. I'll see about assigning one of the guys to her and Nakia."

"Get Hudson. He's great with kids," Trace said as he finished off the breakfast.

Connie didn't know that about Hudson but planned to add that information to his file. Maybe Trinity was right in suggesting they offer Trace a management position. The security team respected and trusted him. He had a different type of relationship with them than she and

Trinity did. A relationship that could prove beneficial when matching security specialists to potential clients.

For the next few minutes, they discussed their plans. Trace suggested that they stay the night with Langston and then make a move the next morning. In the meantime, they needed clothes and toiletries before they relocated to one of LEPA's safe houses.

Connie was used to taking care of logistics for clients. She just never thought that she'd be one of them.

## Chapter 21

The next day, after Trace cleared the safe house, he let Connie inside. They had a state-of-the-art security system in the home that included cameras on the outside of the house, bulletproof windows and heavy-duty locks. Connie wasn't sure why he had to clear the house with all of that in place, but she kept her mouth shut. She appreciated how seriously he was taking the situation.

They had first stopped by his condo so that he could pack a bag and had considered staying there since it was a secured building. After discussing it, though, Trace had decided that she might be safer in a safe house. They didn't know exactly who they were dealing with yet. If Daniel Atkinson was involved or was the person who'd hacked the bank system, they might also know about Trace. He said he wasn't willing to take any chances with her safety. Which was why he had just finished double-checking windows and the security system. Now he was walking around the outside of the property.

Connie strolled through the immaculate three-bedroom, two-bathroom single-level home located in a suburb outside of the city. LEPA owned a few safe houses in the area, but Trinity had discussed selling some of them. So far, they rarely needed them since their clientele mostly preferred staying in their own properties when hiring protection.

She stepped into the master suite and glanced around. She had been responsible for remodeling and furnishing this home. White walls were the backdrop to the brightly decorated room with beige and taupe accents.

Connie hugged herself as she took in her new surroundings. Her home had burned down a couple of days ago. Yet it still seemed unreal. It was as if she was living someone else's nightmare, but that wasn't the case. She was actually homeless. There were moments in the past days that she'd tear up and think about all that she had lost. Telling herself that it was just *stuff* helped for a minute, but the reality spoke louder. That *stuff* was a big part of her life that held so many memories. Some things just weren't replaceable.

*Okay, girl, shake it off.* Connie couldn't allow herself to sink into despair. She'd had enough of that. It was time to come up with a game plan. There was so much to think about. Rebuild? Or buy a new home? The whole process would be like starting her life all over again. Right now, though, she had to stay strong and stay safe.

She glanced in the attached bathroom that was large with a gorgeous soaking tub. Something she definitely planned to use while there. Pulling open the drawers in the vanity, she saw that it was fully stocked with every toiletry they could possibly need.

"Everything is locked down, but there's something we haven't discussed," Trace said when Connie exited the bathroom. He was leaning against the door frame, and he still looked a little tired. Hopefully, he'd get caught up on his sleep while they were there.

"What's that?" She sat on the foot of the bed and kicked off her new tennis shoes. Trinity had done some shopping for her and had clothes and a few other items delivered to Langston's home before they left.

Trace dropped down on the bed, then lay back and stared up at the ceiling. "Sleeping arrangements. How do you want to do this?"

Connie crawled farther onto the bed and propped up on her elbow. "What do you mean?" Staring down at him, she caressed the light stubble on his cheek. He hadn't shaved in a couple of days, but she liked the look. It made him appear even more rugged and badass.

Trace reached over and slid his hand onto her thigh. Not in a sexual type of way, but in a way that let her know that he just wanted to touch her. Connie liked that about him. Even when they were riding in the car, he'd hold her hand or rest his hand on her leg. Anything to be in contact with her. It was comforting.

His eyes drifted closed and for a minute she thought he had fallen asleep.

"I mean, technically, I'm supposed to be guarding

you," he said, his voice low and raspy, the way it had been the day before when he was half-asleep. "I should probably sleep in one of the other bedrooms."

"Why?"

"Because you're a distraction." She tsked, and his eyes popped open. He turned his head slightly and met her gaze. "I mean, a gorgeous distraction."

She smiled down at him and placed a quick kiss on his lips. "Good save, but I still don't understand."

"It's never a good idea for security specialists to guard anyone they're attracted to. It's too easy for situations to get complicated. I don't want there to be a time when I'm curled up with you and someone gets the jump on me. Or catches me unalert. That would be putting us both in jeopardy."

Connie nodded her understanding, but she didn't like the idea of them sleeping in separate rooms. "Well, technically, you took a few days off of work. So even though this is LEPA's property and you're part of their security team, you're not here in an official capacity."

A slow smile tilted the corners of his mouth. "Beautiful and smart. You're right."

"Besides, you saved my life in the middle of the night when I was lying curled up beside you. I guess I wasn't *that* much of a distraction."

"Another good point." He reached up, placed his hand behind her neck and pulled her closer. "Just so we're clear. You're a distraction whenever I'm around you, but that night was all about taking care of my woman. Me getting us out of that house had nothing to do with work or anything like that."

"Well, maybe you should take care of your woman right now. Then again, maybe I should take care of you."

Connie straddled him and covered his mouth with hers. In a matter of days, they'd gone from good friends to lovers. In her heart, though, he meant so much more to her. He had sacrificed so much of himself for her. She kissed him with passion, wanting him to feel how much she cared for him…how much she loved him.

Connie wasn't sure when her feelings had blossomed into something that was so strong and satisfying. But for the first time in her life, she wasn't going to over-think the excitement he always sparked inside her. No. This time she was going to let nature take its course and enjoy the ride.

The next day, Connie paced the length of the bedroom, trying to drum up enough courage to call her father. How crazy was that? This was a man who reached out to her a few times a week, just because. Yet she rarely talked to him, often allowing him to go to voice mail. Or she'd answer and end up cutting the conversation short, claiming to be busy. Sure, her days were usually swamped, but not too busy that she couldn't take time to talk to him.

She was so disappointed in herself. If the past week had taught her anything, it was that life was short and often unpredictable. It could change in an instant, as was her experience lately. It was way past time for her to quit acting childish and rebuild a relationship with her parents, but especially her father. No one was promised tomorrow. It would break her heart if something happened to him before she had a chance to strengthen their bond.

It wasn't just the fire and Richard's murder that had her thinking about her dad. It was also her relationship with Trace. More than anything, Connie wanted it to last. There was a better chance at that if she repaired the relationship with her father. Otherwise, would she really be able to have a fulfilling future with Trace?

She dialed her father's number, and the phone rang three times before he picked up.

"Hello."

Hearing the cheery voice did something to her. The ache she'd been feeling in her heart since watching her home turn to rubble eased a bit.

"Hi, Dad," she said and bit down on her lip to keep from sobbing. She'd cried more in the past week than she had cried in years. When had she gotten to be so emotional?

"Tiny?" he said, using her childhood nickname. "Is that you?"

"Hi, Dad. Yeah, it's me."

"Sweetheart, is everything okay? You don't usually call, especially this time of day," he said in a rush, worry in his tone.

How sad was it that he assumed something was wrong since she didn't call often? Connie had sworn her sister to secrecy, so she knew her dad didn't know anything about what was going on.

"Everything is okay. You were on my mind, and I figured I'd call you."

After a slight hesitation, he said, "It's so good to hear your voice. God, I've missed you."

"I've missed you, too, Dad," she said honestly. She hadn't wanted another day to go by without letting him know that she loved him. Her parents wouldn't be around forever. It didn't matter what had happened in the past. All that mattered was what they did from that day forward.

"What have you been up to?" he asked, and Connie almost laughed. Not because she had anything to laugh about, but sometimes you had to laugh to keep from crying.

She sat in the wide upholstered chair and curled her legs beneath her. Then she told him some of what had been going on during the past week. Not wanting him to worry, she kept the gang stuff, Mr. Gray Eyes, Daniel Atkinson and the arson out of the story. All he knew was that she was at a bank that got robbed and her home fire was being investigated.

"Are you sure you're all right? Where are you staying? Are you with Erica or Trinity?"

"No, actually. I'm in temporary housing. At least until I figure out next steps."

"Oh, all right. Well, if you ever want to get out of town for a while, you know you're welcome here. We have room and would love to have you."

"I'll take you up on that in the near future. Right now, though, I need to get situated here. Did I ever tell you that I work at Trinity's personal-security company?"

"I heard, but you don't just work there. Erica said

that you're the VP of Operations and that you run the whole company."

Connie laughed. She loved the pride she heard in his voice and could almost imagine him puffing out his chest and saying, "My daughter, the VP."

He might not have been good husband material for her mom, but in all honesty, he'd been a good dad. Up until he moved out of the country, he'd been the one to help with homework, attend PTA meetings and had even gone on a few field trips with her class. Funny how Connie hadn't thought of any of that in the last twenty years.

She told him about the job and how much she enjoyed it.

"Sounds like you're keeping yourself busy. What about your social life? Are you dating?" he asked.

An involuntary smile spread across her mouth. "Yes, I am, and he's a wonderful man. His name is Trace and he used to be in the navy. Now he works for LEPA. You'd like him, especially since he has your sense of humor."

He laughed, probably thinking about all the jokes he used to tell her and Erica when they were growing up.

"I hope to meet him one day. Actually, I'll be in California at the end of the year. Maybe, if you're still dating him, I can meet him then."

"Okay. Just make sure you let me know ahead of time, and we'll meet you there. Or, if you can, maybe you can spend some time in Vegas while you're in the country."

"I'll make time. You're my baby girl. Just because

we don't talk often doesn't mean that I don't love you. That goes for your sister and Nakia, too. You girls are my heart."

"I love you, Dad," she blurted, aching to get those words out. Connie didn't want another day to go by without him knowing that she really did love him. "I'm sorry I haven't done a better job at keeping in touch."

"Oh, sweetheart, it's okay. There are a lot of things I'm sorry for and things I wish I could do over. I know it was hard on you girls when your mom and I couldn't get our act together. I never meant to hurt you guys. I don't know if you know this, but your mother and I have made peace."

"Really?" Connie couldn't believe what she was hearing. How had she missed that?

Her dad laughed. "Yes, *really*. I know it's hard to believe, but now that we're older and wiser, we've been able to leave the past in the past. Did you know she was married again?"

Now Connie was the one laughing at how surprised he sounded. "Yeah, I guess third time's a charm…or is it four times now? I can't keep up, but she finally seems happy."

"Yes, she does. That's all I've ever wanted for both of us. Actually, for all of us. Sweetheart, I'm really glad you called. You know, your sister calls me at least once a week."

Connie grinned. "Is that right?"

"Yes, and maybe you can call me a little more often than you do now. Or I can call you."

"I plan to do better, Dad, but you can always call me whenever you want. Do you have a computer?"

"Yes."

"Then maybe me, you and Erica can video-chat sometimes."

"That sounds great! I'd love to see you girls, but you'll probably have to walk me through it. I'm not really into all of this tech stuff."

They talked for a few minutes longer before ending the call, and Connie felt encouraged that they were on the right track in mending their relationship. She didn't expect everything to be perfect, but as long as her father knew that she loved him and there were no hard feelings, it was a good place to start.

## Chapter 22

Connie was going crazy with being cooped up in the safe house for the last few days. Her patience had never been that great, and knowing that the authorities hadn't located Daniel Atkinson wasn't helping. The only thing that was keeping her going was talking to her sister every day and being at the house with Trace, even though lately she was probably getting on his nerves.

"I don't know how people deal with having someone shadow them 24/7. This type of life is not for me," Erica said.

"Yeah, me, either." Connie loved her job and was glad the company could provide a needed service, but her sister was right. Having someone constantly in your face for the main purpose of keeping you safe took some getting used to.

Thankfully, the setup was a little different for her and Trace. He was staying vigilant, but their time at the house was giving them a chance to get to know each other better. That was good for the most part, but Connie was getting frustrated with all of the waiting.

"I might be tired of my human shadow," Erica continued, "but Nakia is crazy about Hudson. I have to give him credit. He's extremely patient with her, trying to make it seem normal that he's hanging around."

Her niece loved everyone, but Connie couldn't deny that Hudson was one of the good ones. Their gentle giant was how Trinity referred to him. Hudson had played one year in the NFL, but then a kneecap injury ended his career. Considering he used to tackle people for a living, and the football league considered him one of the most dangerous players on the field, his soft-spoken manner was disarming. He had a kind and easygoing personality as long as he wasn't crossed.

Connie had only witnessed one time when he snapped, and that had been when he was accused of stealing from a client. The client had threatened to get the police involved. Hudson had been livid. He didn't calm down until Connie assured him that she and Trinity believed him.

Days later, the client had called to say that they'd made a mistake. Their drug-addicted son had stolen the jewelry. When he called months later, requesting another security specialist to travel with him, they'd decided that LEPA wasn't a good fit for his needs. They took protecting their clients seriously, but Trinity had created a family-like environment for everyone who worked for her. Supporting and backing their team came first.

"So how are things with you and the stallion?"

"Stallion? Really?" Connie laughed, something she realized she hadn't been doing much of lately. "That's what we're calling him now?"

"Hey, with the way you describe him, I picture this amazingly powerful, virile man who can't be tamed."

Connie thought about that for a minute. Amazing, powerfully built and virile...yes. But *untamable* probably wasn't a good word. She would never try controlling Trace. Besides, she would never have to. He was the perfect gentleman, and always conscious of her feelings and needs.

"He's great," Connie said, instead of sharing everything she was thinking. "I don't know how I would've gotten through this past week and a half without him."

"I'm glad he's been there for you. I'm still looking forward to meeting him. Hopefully, we can all get together for dinner or something soon."

Connie smiled. It had been a long time since she had introduced anyone she was dating to her sister. Before Kevin died, he and Erica would invite Connie over for dinner all the time. They occasionally tried to fix her up on blind dates, but after one of the men they introduced her to ended up getting arrested during the date, they stopped.

"I guess I should've asked. How are you holding up? Any more issues with the mystery man?"

"Mommy, Hudson said he'd take us to get ice cream if we want. Can we?" Nakia begged in the background.

Erica sighed loudly, but Connie heard something else in her tone. Whimsy? Playfulness? Erica wasn't a big sweet eater and rarely gave in to Nakia's whims. Could it be that her sister was enjoying Hudson's company more than she was letting on?

"So, you and Hudson?" Connie asked cautiously.

"Don't start. He's nice and he's sweet to my kid. Besides all of that, he's keeping us safe."

"Uh-huh, and you *like* him." Connie didn't bother pointing out the fact that Erica hadn't said no to the idea of her and Hudson. It had been two years since Kevin's death. Connie would love to see her sibling meet a nice guy and live happily ever after. If anyone needed a happy ending, it was Erica.

"Okay, sis. I'm outnumbered," Erica said. "Gotta go. You stay safe and call me tomorrow."

"Will do, and have fun," Connie teased before hanging up.

She glanced at the time. They'd been on the phone for an hour. She wondered what Trace was up to. Normally, he would've checked in on her by now.

She tossed her phone onto the bed as a plan formed in her head. Since she'd been kind of a pain complaining about everything lately, she wanted to do something special for him. Maybe after she fixed them a nice dinner, she'd put on a little striptease show for him.

Connie strolled out of the bedroom and headed to the front of the house, but froze in the middle of the hallway. Whoever Trace was on the phone with had him laughing and talking loudly. Deciding to give him some privacy, she turned to go back into the bedroom.

"Dude, are you kidding me? Don't call me with some nonsense. Just call me VP of Operations," Trace said, and Connie stopped.

Dread tore through her body and nipped at her nerves. VP of Operations? That was her position at LEPA.

The night before, she had suggested to Trace that he consider taking on a management role with LEPA. He told her he wasn't really interested, but would think about it. Surely, he wasn't thinking about her position. Was he? Was he after her job?

"Yeah, right. Whatever," Trace said to the caller. "I already know Trinity will go along with whatever I suggest. Besides, I already have big plans for the position," he continued, laughing as if it was some big joke.

Shock and anger warred inside Connie as she stomped back to the bedroom. She'd been the VP of Operations at LEPA since moving to Las Vegas over a year ago. There was no way Trinity would strip her of the title or the position, especially not without talking to her first.

Then again, Trinity had known Trace since they were kids. He was like a brother to her. Not only that, but he could also easily do the job. He had the educational background, knew the company just as well if not better than she did, and everyone loved him.

*No. No. No.*

There had to be an explanation. There was no way they'd do this to her. But as she played back some of their recent conversations, it all led back to the same thing. Trace wanted the VP job. Her VP job! He had said himself that he didn't want to provide personal security anymore. Now she understood why he didn't seem all that interested when she suggested he take on a management position at LEPA.

He already had a plan in the works.

*How could he do this to me?*

Was that why he had pursued her so hard over the last few months? So that he could one day swoop in and take her job? This was the Quincy situation all over again, but worse. She thought she'd been in love with Quincy, but what she felt for Trace went beyond anything she had ever experienced.

"How could he?"

He knew what had happened between her and Quincy. How could he betray her like this?

"No. Not this time."

This time she wouldn't let a man get away with stabbing her in the back. This time she'd fight. Her experience with Quincy should've taught her to never mix business with pleasure. This was why she had rules: no dating coworkers.

Connie plopped down on the bed and grabbed the laptop Trinity had sent over the other day. The first thing she needed to do was find a new security specialist. She might be mad enough to leave the house and look out for herself until the gray-eyed bastard was caught, but she wasn't stupid. It wouldn't take much to assign someone else to her.

She looked at everyone's accounts to see who was available. They were in the market for more specialists thanks to business picking up, but there had to be someone free.

Connie perused the database and saw that Riley had

finished a short assignment a couple of days ago. Like Trace, he was a popular choice. But what made Riley a popular choice was not only his good looks, but also that he was bilingual.

She shot off a quick text, telling him she needed him on the job immediately for a few days. Within minutes, he responded.

No problem. I'll be there in twenty.

Connie stayed in the bedroom until she heard the doorbell. When she got to the living room, Riley was there with a duffel bag hanging on his shoulder.

"You said Connie contacted you?" Trace asked him. Connie cleared her throat and he turned to her, confusion in his eyes. "What do you need Riley for?"

"I'm releasing you of your duties. Riley is taking over my detail."

"Why?" Trace asked, his intense eyes searching hers.

Her heart cracked a little inside her chest. It didn't matter that he hurt her; she still loved him and that made her angrier.

Tears pooled in her eyes but she blinked them back. "I think it's best that I have a new security detail." Riley entered and she said, "Thanks for coming so quickly. I'll show you to your room."

Trace got in front of her and blocked her view. "I don't know what's going on, but I'm not going anywhere until we talk."

"We don't have anything—"

"Riley, can you step outside and give us a minute?" Trace asked, his eyes squarely on Connie.

"Don't go anywhere, Riley," she demanded.

"Clearly, you two have things to work out. I'll be sitting on the patio out back. Connie, holler if you need me." He walked past them and Connie didn't miss the way he glared at Trace.

"What's going on?" Trace asked in a clipped tone. He had always been patient with her, but the way he was glaring clearly showed she was pushing his limits.

"What's going on is that you and I are done. You know the way out."

Connie turned on her heel and started back to the bedroom, but realized he'd have to go in there for his clothes. She went to the hall bathroom instead. When she tried closing the door, Trace was right there.

"I'm not going anywhere until you tell me what the hell I did wrong."

# Chapter 23

Connie shoved past him and went back to the bedroom that they'd been sharing, and Trace followed her. How could she have let herself fall in love with him? Men. Even at her age, she still managed to pick wrong.

"Tell me what is going on. How you gon' just call Riley up to replace me, especially without letting me know?" His voice rose with each word, and Connie couldn't ever remember seeing him so angry. She didn't feel threatened, but he'd caught her off guard.

"I told you about Quincy and how he stabbed me in the back. Then he accepted a job that should've been mine."

Trace stared at her, then gave a slight shrug. "Yeah, and? What does that have to do with you and me? What does that have to do with you calling Riley?"

Connie sighed loudly with her hands planted firmly on her hips. "Trace, I heard you."

"Sweetheart, you heard what? What did you hear?" he demanded.

"I heard you telling someone that the VP of Operations position was yours. There is no way Trinity is giving you *my* job, but the fact that you think she's going to go along with whatever stupid plan you've cooked up—"

"Hold up!" His face contorted with confusion. "You think I'm after *your* job? Why the hell would I go after your job, Connie? There is nobody better suited for that position. Besides, I don't have the tolerance for the crap you have to deal with every day."

"But—but you said—"

"You heard me talking to Langston about our PI business."

Her eyebrows bunched together as she tried to figure out what he was talking about. "What PI business?"

"The PI business that he and I are planning to start. We were joking around about job titles, and I just threw that out there. Hell, we don't even need titles. We were just clowning around. As for Trinity, we're thinking about seeing how we can partner up or collaborate or something with LEPA."

Guilt stabbed Connie in the chest, then twisted her insides. "Oh."

*"Oh?"* He got in her face. "Oh? That's all you have to say? You think so little of me that you accuse me of trying to take your job? I'm not Quincy. I have worked my ass off to be a good man!" He pounded his chest

and his words were filled with so much anguish that tears filled Connie's eyes.

"I've tried to be the best version of myself that I can be. Yet here we are, having a conversation I never thought we'd have. I'm not playing some damn game with you, and I sure as hell ain't playing with your feelings. I love you and would *never* do anything to hurt you."

"I love you, too, and I'm so sorry for accusing you."

Connie didn't know what else to say. What could she say? She'd automatically assumed the worst based on her experience. It didn't matter if it was past experience. All she had to go on was how she'd been treated in the past.

*That's not true*, that little voice inside her head said.

From day one, even when they were just friends and getting to know each other, Trace had been kind. He treated her better than any man had ever treated her, and she didn't doubt his feelings. Yet she'd been quick to think the worst.

Regret lodged in her throat. She'd always had a bad habit of jumping to conclusions. She should know by now that things weren't always how they seemed.

"And what does your accusation say about Trinity?" Trace continued. "Do you honestly think she'd snatch *your* job from you to give to *me*? It doesn't matter how long she and I have known each other. She would *never* do anything like that."

"I know," Connie said quietly, feeling awful that she would think the worst of people whom she loved more than anything.

*"You know?* Yet you thought the worst of her and me." Trace ran his hand over his head and let it slide to the back of his neck. "I can't do this. You and I might not be a good idea after all. I love you, but I can't be with someone who doesn't trust me."

"Honey, I love you, too," she said quickly, fisting the front of his T-shirt and holding on tight to keep him from walking away. "And I trust you. I trust you more than I trust anybody. I guess I—I—I don't have a good excuse for my reaction. My active imagination went from zero to sixty in a heartbeat, and I am so sorry. You're right. You're not Quincy. Deep in my heart—" she placed a hand on her chest "—I know I can trust you, and I do. I really do. Please forgive me."

He stood near the door, studying her for the longest time. All Connie could do was stand there. She held her breath, hoping she hadn't just screwed up the best thing that had ever happened to her.

"I forgive you, but I think it's best that Riley take over."

"Trace, please don't leave."

Connie didn't know what else to say as he emptied the drawers and tossed his clothes into his bag.

The heaviness in her chest was almost suffocating as her heart crumbled into tiny pieces. She didn't blame him for wanting to leave. She deserved to be alone.

Connie watched him grab his clothes and shove them into his leather duffel bag. Less than five minutes, and he was ready to leave.

"Trace, please don't go."

He stepped to her and slowly pushed a lock of hair behind her ear. Hope blossomed inside her. Maybe he really did forgive her. Maybe he'd give her another chance to get things right between them.

Trace slid his hand to the back of her neck and pulled her closer. Relief flooded Connie until he surprised her and placed a lingering kiss on her forehead. Not her cheek. Not her lips. But her forehead.

It was over.

They were done.

He was moving on.

When Trace dropped his hand and stepped back, the hurt in his eyes was almost her undoing. She would never forgive herself for accusing him. How could she have been so careless? How could she doubt him even for a minute when, in her heart, she trusted him more than she trusted anyone?

"Take care of yourself," he said quietly.

Watching him walk out of the room and out of her life was like taking a butcher knife to the heart. Every nerve inside Connie went numb. Trace hadn't been just her man. He was also one of her best friends. Now he was gone.

*What have I done?*

# Chapter 24

The last few days had been hell, Trace thought. He hadn't realized just how much Connie had become a part of him until the day after he walked out of the safe house. Since then, everything seemed duller. Quieter. Life wasn't as fulfilling as it had been with her.

As he sat in his living room, playing his saxophone, the rich, sharp melody seeped into his soul, filling the emptiness in his heart. The last notes of Sam Smith's "Stay with Me" flowed right into Whitney Houston's version of "I Will Always Love You."

Trace closed his eyes and poured everything he was feeling into the instrumental. Love. Loss. Pain. Heartache. He knew he needed to get himself together and pull out of this slump. That was why he'd picked up his sax. Sorting out his feelings with music had always helped clear his head.

Connie was vulnerable. He knew that, especially after all that she'd been through lately, but her accusation cut deep. Trace hadn't given her any reason to doubt him. He definitely hadn't given her a reason to think that he'd stoop so low and go after her job. It pissed him off all over again just thinking about it. But he still loved her. He still wanted her in his life. He just didn't know how to help her move on from past hurts.

He played the last verse of the song and didn't stop even when his alarm system signaled he had company. Trace already knew it could only be one of a few people walking into his home without ringing the bell. Just as he hit a high note, his visitors came into view. Langston and Maxwell stood on the edge of the family room, looking at him as if he had two heads.

"Well, at least he's gotten better at playing that thing," Maxwell said and set two shopping bags on the dining table.

Langston just stared at Trace as if seeing him for the first time. Once the song ended, his brother started clapping. "I'll have to tell the family that you finally learned how to play," he said and dropped down on the leather sectional.

Trace unhooked his saxophone from the strap and set the instrument back in its stand without commenting.

"It's bad enough I had to work a double," Langston continued and stretched out his legs before folding his arms across his chest. "But to get a call telling me that your ass is missing made the day that much longer."

"Well, as you can see, I'm not missing. So who sent out the distress signal that has you both invading my privacy?"

"Trinity," they said in unison.

"I should've known."

Trace had left her a voice mail telling her that he was resigning his position at LEPA. Though a small part of his decision had to do with his relationship with Connie, she hadn't been his sole reason. It was time for him to move on from security work and start his own business. He had enough money saved up to live comfortably for at least a year. Included with his verbal resignation, he had told Trinity that he'd be available to fill in on occasion when she couldn't find anyone else.

As for him and Connie, Trace wasn't giving up on their relationship. He had just needed a few days to regroup and make sure she was who he wanted to be with. He knew without a doubt that he didn't want anyone else.

Maxwell pulled a six-pack of beer out of one of the bags, along with chips, dip and a host of other junk food. He handed a beer to Langston and then tossed one to Trace before sitting in the leather recliner near the window.

"Why are you guys really here?" Trace asked.

"I'm here because your neighbors called in complaints about noise coming from your unit," Maxwell said with a straight face, but his lips started twitching. "They're expecting me to give you a citation."

"And I'm here to make sure you're alive."

"Well, I'm alive, and I'll stop making noise. I guess

that means you two can leave. Oh, and before you go, leave my house key on the table. It was supposed to be for emergency use only."

Langston's eyebrows drew together and he glared at Trace. "This was an emergency. Now quit being a jerk."

"Fight nice, guys." Maxwell took a long drag on his beer. "Since I don't have any plans for the evening, I was thinking we can play poker. I figure since Trace is all up in his feelings, I might be able to win a hand or two and take his money."

That made Trace laugh. Considering Maxwell's best friend was a professional poker player, Max couldn't play worth a damn.

"I ain't that down-and-out. There's no way you're taking my money. Unless you brought Gunner with you, I'll be a little richer before…"

The intercom buzzed, and Langston burst out laughing.

Maxwell stood and walked over to the intercom with a stupid grin on his face. "Hmm… I wonder who that can be."

A few minutes later, Gunner strolled in with his traveling poker gear and set up everything on Trace's table. They played several hands before one of them brought up Connie. Trace shot down that conversation quick. He'd been thinking about her nonstop but wasn't ready to discuss what had happened between them.

"Did I ever tell you guys about the time Trinity tried to leave me?" Gunner asked.

Everyone around the table groaned. Gunner wasn't a big talker, but when he did, he went on and on and on.

"It was when we first started dating and it was during one of the biggest poker tournaments of the year. Trinity hated the fact that I was a gambler, and it didn't matter that I was a *professional* poker player. She couldn't understand the importance of me needing to keep my head in the game."

Maxwell threw a couple of poker chips into the center of the table. "I'll raise you twenty, and Gunner, man, is this story going anywhere?"

"I was losing at this point in the tournament," Gunner continued, as if Maxwell hadn't said anything. "I couldn't get focused. So I had to put some mental distance between me and Trinity." He gave a mock shiver and grimaced, and Trace laughed. "You guys know what a hothead that woman is. She wanted my undivided attention even though there were millions of dollars at stake.

"Anyway, the tournament was here in town, but we were staying at the host hotel. By the third or the fourth night of me practically ignoring her so that I could get my head on straight, she'd had enough. She told me she was going home—back to LA—and was planning to leave my ass in the hotel."

"What did you do?" Trace asked. He could totally see Trinity cutting out and not looking back.

"I let her go," Gunner said, sticking his chest out like he was the man. "I gave her the keys to the car and said, 'See ya.'"

"Man, quit fronting." Maxwell laughed. "You let her go for about five minutes. Then you called the hotel's concierge and had them stop her in the lobby. It was too late, though. Trinity was already in his car revving the engine."

"Not just any car. Get it right if you're going to butt in to my story."

"Okay, his precious, overpriced BMW sports car," Maxwell said, making a face as if to say "big deal." "Anyway, Gunner had to run after her and jump into the passenger seat. Long story short, they ended up getting chased by some guy who was trying to kill Gunner, and you both know how Trinity drives. She had them flying down secluded roads and hugging curves on two wheels."

Gunner shook his head. "Scared the crap out of me. I thought we were going to die, but there was no other place I wanted to be than with her."

Trace could only imagine how that ride went. Trinity was trained in defensive driving, but even before she became a cop, she'd driven like she was trying out for NASCAR.

"Okay, maybe it's just me, but what the hell is the point of this story?" Langston asked, frowning.

Trace and Maxwell burst out laughing, but after a while, Trace turned serious.

"The point is, even though he and Trinity were mad at each other, he refused to let her walk out of his life. Ride or die," Trace explained.

"That woman was and still is my heartbeat," Gunner said to all of them, but his gaze was on Trace. "That tournament and the ones that followed meant nothing if she wasn't in my life. I couldn't just let her walk away and risk never seeing her again. I *had* to go after her.

I had to make sure she knew that she was it for me, no matter what."

Trace nodded. His and Connie's situation was a little different, but that was how he felt. He didn't know how to get past her defenses. All he could do was love her unconditionally and hang on for the ride.

"Thanks for that, Gunner. I get it. I'm not giving up my woman. And all I have to say to you two—" he glanced at his brother and Maxwell "—is that you're useless. If you're going to come over and give a pep talk, at least come with a story like Gunner did."

"Man, forget you." Langston waved him off and started moving around the cards in his hand. "I already told you that I only came over to make sure you were alive."

Maxwell's cell phone, which was sitting on the table next to him, rang. He glanced at the screen, then hurried and answered.

"Yeah, this is Max."

Trace could only hear one side of the conversation, but whoever his friend was talking to was giving him some good news.

"All right, thanks for letting me know." He disconnected the call and smiled at Trace. "They got him," he said.

Trace stared, trying not to get too excited. "Who? Daniel Atkinson?"

"Yep. They got a tip from a caller that said he and two other guys were hiding out in Boulder City at some woman's house. They picked them up a little while ago."

"Are they sure one of them is Atkinson? Gray eyes, tat and—"

"It's him, and they're confident that they can break

the other two, get them to turn on each other. But we're going to want Connie to come to the station and see if she can pick Atkinson out of a lineup. Oh, and it helped a lot that you and Langston were able to figure out that he was part of the One-Seven Crew."

Trace was cautiously optimistic that the chaos that had become part of his life was over. But now, what to do about Connie?

Later that night, Trace was sitting on his balcony when his cell phone rang. Unease swept through him when he saw that it was Riley. His friend had been doing a good job keeping him up-to-date on how Connie was doing, but rarely did he call this late.

"Is she all right?" Trace asked by way of greeting.

"You'd know how she is if you had bothered to answer her calls over the last few days."

"Just tell me!" Trace snapped, his heart rate amping up as his concern for Connie increased. "Is she okay?"

"Besides not eating or sleeping, she's fine."

Trace massaged his temples, trying to tamp down his anxiety. Connie couldn't have weighed more than a hundred and ten pounds. She couldn't afford to not eat.

"She wants me to go to the police station with her tomorrow."

That surprised Trace. She rarely asked anyone for anything, and now that Daniel was in custody, Trace was surprised that she wasn't trying to get rid of Riley.

"Good. I think it's a good idea that she doesn't go alone."

"Trace, man, I get that you're pissed about whatever went down with you two. Clearly, it was something she did, because she said something about you never being able to forgive her. But whatever happened, it's not worth seeing her miserable. You've been acting like an asshole—Trinity's words, not mine—and I'm thinking this might be a chance for you to patch things up."

"How so?" Trace asked, wondering where the conversation was headed.

"Instead of me taking her to the police station, you take her. That'll give her a chance to apologize since that's what she's been trying to do, but you keep dodging her calls."

Trace huffed out a long, exhausted breath and stared into the night. Sitting on the balcony reminded him of the first night that Connie had stayed at his place. She loved it out there. Now, whenever he hung out on the balcony, it was impossible not to think of her.

"All right. You drive her to the police station, and I'll meet her there."

The next day, Trace stood near the help desk at the police station waiting for Connie. What a difference a couple of weeks made. It was like déjà vu, being back there. They'd been through a lot since the bank robbery, and it was over.

*Almost*, he reminded himself. It was almost over. He wouldn't be totally comfortable until Atkinson was behind bars for life.

Trace glanced at his watch. Connie would be there in a few minutes. He had mixed feelings about seeing her. Part of him wanted to pull her into his arms and never let go. The other part of him knew he needed to tread lightly. They needed to talk and figure out if they were going to give their relationship another shot.

Left up to him, it would be a no-brainer. But he needed to see where her head was at.

Trace glanced at the door just as Connie walked in. She didn't look his way, which gave him a chance to get his fill of her. Her hair was hanging down around her shoulders, and she was casually dressed in a yellow short-sleeved blouse and navy blue pants. Her signature high-heeled shoes covered her feet.

As if sensing him staring, she glanced his way and her eyes grew round. He already knew Riley hadn't told her he'd be there, and he was glad he could surprise her. She had definitely lost weight, and the dark circles under her eyes were proof of lack of sleep. Despite that, though, she was still the most beautiful woman he'd ever seen.

"Trace," she said on a breath, but didn't make a move toward him. She folded her lower lip between her teeth and her eyes searched his. It was as if she was trying to decide what to do or say.

"Hey, sweetheart," he said, pushing off the wall and moving toward her. She met him halfway and launched herself into his arms.

"I've missed you so much," she mumbled against his neck.

"Not as much as I've missed you. Damn… I've missed you like crazy."

"I am so sorry for everything," she said. When Trace set her on her feet, she reached for his hand. "I never meant to hurt you. Can you ever forgive me?"

"I already have." He had told her that before leaving the safe house that day. Yet, considering he hadn't answered any of her calls, she had every right to doubt that he really meant it. "We'll talk more later."

"Okay, but what are you doing here?"

He pushed her hair out of her face and cupped her soft cheek. "I didn't want you to go through this by yourself."

Connie leaned into his touch and her eyes drifted closed for a minute. When she looked at him again, Trace's heart flipped inside his chest. The love glimmering in her beautiful hazel eyes told him everything he needed to know. She was his, and he was hers.

"Thank you for being here for me. I know I don't deserve you, but if you feel anything for me…will you give me another chance?"

Trace studied her, his heart bursting with love, and he nodded. "Definitely. It's you and me, baby."

He lowered his head and kissed her sweet lips. All the anguish from the last few days drifted into the background. He kissed her hard and thoroughly, wanting her to feel how much he loved her. Wanting her to feel how much he had missed her. Sure, they had things to work out, but he was confident that they would get through this rough patch.

When the kiss ended, all he wanted to do was carry her out of there, but she had a job to do.

"You ready to help put a bad guy behind bars?"

She nodded. "I'm ready. Let's do this."

## Chapter 25

Connie danced in her theater seat and mouthed the words to the song that the actress was singing. She had first seen this classic Broadway show the one time she had visited New York. Since then, she tried to get tickets to it whenever the show was in Las Vegas or Los Angeles.

"Exactly how many times have you seen this production?" Trace whispered close to her ear.

She grinned at him and lifted both of her hands, signaling that she'd seen it ten times. He shook his head and smirked. She didn't bother telling him that Erica had probably seen it twice as many times.

Trace reached over and interlocked his hand with hers and Connie smiled. They had reconciled almost a week ago…and this was their first official date. She never knew she could love someone as much as she loved this man. Those few days that they'd been apart had given her time to do some soul-searching. Being separated from him had almost broken her, though. Watching him leave the safe house that day had felt like a part of her heart had walked out the door with him. But after a long talk over dinner the night after she had ID'd Daniel Atkinson, she was confident that they could make their relationship work.

"How long is this show?" Trace whispered.

Connie grinned. "We just got here. You can't be tired of it yet." His left eyebrow lifted as if to say "you wanna bet?"

An hour into the show, Connie's leg bounced up and down as she debated whether to make a quick run to the ladies' room or wait until intermission. But there wasn't a woman alive who didn't know what to expect at that point. It didn't matter how many bathroom stalls the building had; it was guaranteed that there would be a line for women.

She'd wait until ten minutes before intermission. At least then, if a line had formed already, it wouldn't be too long.

*I really have to use the bathroom*, Connie thought as she squeezed her thighs together and checked her watch. She was worse than a little kid trying to *hold it*.

Trace put his arm around her, resting it on the back of her seat, then leaned in. "What's wrong?"

Connie shook her head. Did the man miss anything? It was amazing how tuned in he was to her. Then again, she had been wiggling in her seat.

She leaned close to his ear. "I need to go to the bathroom."

"Well, let's go," he said, as if it wasn't a big deal.

Connie didn't want him to miss any of the show since he hadn't seen it before. But she knew him well enough to know that he wouldn't let her walk out by herself. It didn't matter that Daniel Atkinson was in custody and being charged with murder, as well as armed robbery. Trace was overprotective by nature.

"Okay," she said.

They stood, and Trace held her hand as they quietly stepped over people, whispering "excuse me" along the way. Thankfully they were close to the end of the row and didn't have to cross in front of too many people.

Once they were in the foyer, they headed down the extra-wide, semispiraled staircase that took them to the lower level. Connie suggested Trace get them a drink before intermission. That way they could beat the crowd and long lines.

"Okay, but meet me right here in seven minutes," he insisted.

Connie laughed. "Seriously? How do you know I don't need more time than that?"

Trace slipped his large hand behind her neck and pulled her to him. "Seven minutes and not a minute longer." He gave her a quick kiss on the lips. "Now hurry up."

"All right. I'll be back."

Connie speed-walked to the other end of the long foyer, humming the song that the actors were singing when she and Trace walked out. She couldn't remember being as happy as she'd been over the last few days. Even being told that her house wasn't structurally safe and would need to be demolished hadn't put a damper on her mood. For now, she had worked it out with Trinity and would rent the safe house for as long as she needed.

Connie hurried into the ladies' room and took care of business. Once done, she stood at the sink washing her hands and checked herself out in the mirror. Her hair was still in place, but her lipstick could use a touch-up. By the time she was finished primping, her time was up.

"I guess I wasn't the only one who wanted to beat the rush, huh?" a woman said as she burst into the bathroom.

Connie smiled. "Nope. Great minds think alike. Enjoy the rest of the show."

"Thanks—you, too."

Connie stepped out of the ladies' room, but stopped and glanced around. She didn't recall there being a wall to her right, and the area was more secluded than she remembered.

"What the…?" She glanced back at the door she had come out of and realized she must've exited out a different way.

She shook her head. Her sense of direction needed work, and she needed to hurry. Otherwise, Trace was going to come looking for her.

Connie hadn't taken three steps before she was pushed hard in the back. She gasped, and before she could get her hands up to brace for impact, the side of her head slammed into a wall.

Pain shot through her skull.

Stars floated in front of her eyes.

Her knees went weak.

Dazed, with her head pounding and her face throbbing, she blinked several times to get her bearings. She didn't have a chance to react when strong arms snaked around her waist and hauled her off the floor.

Whoever it was wasn't Trace. She knew his touch, knew his scent.

Panic roared through her body.

Connie screamed, but a hand slapped over her mouth.

*"No! Let me go! Let me go!"* she screamed, not caring that her words were muffled.

She kicked her legs. Swung her arms. Anything to get away. The person was too strong, but she wouldn't give up. Her arms rotated like helicopter propellers as she twisted, kicked and wiggled, praying that someone would see the struggle.

"Stop it!" The man jerked her and growled in her ear. Then he spun her around, and Connie's heart stopped.

*It can't be.*

*Daniel Atkinson?*

His gray eyes sparked, and he flashed an evil grin. *"Surprise.* I told you I'd see you again."

Connie kicked, aiming for his privates, but he moved and she made contact with his leg. Still, it caught him off guard. She took off and tried to run away, but he was too fast.

"Hel—" she screamed, but he covered her mouth again and lifted her off the floor.

Her heart thumped violently inside her chest, but

she kept wiggling in his arms. Despite her struggling against him, he dragged her toward an exit. Connie used all of her strength to keep twisting and turning, anything to make it hard for him to carry her. He might kill her inside the theater, but if he got her outside, she was as good as dead.

If she just held on a little longer, Trace would be there. The thought of him made her fight harder as tears blurred her vision. She couldn't let this man take her.

Trace strolled through the vestibule, his shoes silent on the multicolored carpet. He had only been to this particular theater twice, but never for a Broadway show. He thought about how Connie had seen the show ten times and wondered what the draw was. Sure, the music and singing were decent, but *ten times*?

He shook his head. Nothing, no type of entertainment, was enjoyable enough for him to see it that often. Even reruns of boxing matches couldn't keep his interest enough to see more than once, and that was one of his favorite sports. But if his baby was happy, that was all that mattered.

Langston had called him *whipped*. That was what he was when it came to her, and damn if it didn't feel good. Taking a step back to take their time in getting to know each other had been the best decision. More than ever, he was looking forward to a future with her.

His phone vibrated in his pocket. He started not to answer it, but figured he could at least check to see who was calling. He glanced at the screen.

*Maxwell.*

Instead of going to the bar, Trace stepped off to the side and answered. "Hello."

"We have a situation," Maxwell said by way of greeting. "Daniel Atkinson has a twin. An identical twin brother."

"Wait. What?" Trace said, trying to figure out what his friend was talking about.

"There's two of them, Trace. Daniel and his brother David. Daniel is the one in custody and affiliated with the One-Seven gang. His brother is probably the one you had words with at the fashion show."

Trace's heart hammered against his chest as he turned and headed back the way he'd come. Connie might not be in danger, but he'd feel better if he had eyes on her.

"He's scum," Maxwell continued. "A couple of years ago, murder charges were brought up on David in Oakland, but the DA couldn't make the charges stick. Now there's a warrant out in Los Angeles for his arrest on another incident, which might be why he's been pretending to be his brother and using Daniel's name. Anyway, keep Connie close because the guy is accused of sexual assault and assault with a deadly weapon."

"I gotta go." Trace ended the call and took off in a run toward the ladies' room. He wanted to believe that Connie was fine, but he wouldn't be comfortable until he saw for himself.

The closer he got to the area, the more his anxiety amped up. He was just about to plow into the restroom when the door swung open, and a woman walked out.

She gasped and her hand went to her chest. "Oh, my God. You scared me."

"Did you see a lady in there? Cute. Long curly hair and a little shorter than you?"

"Uh, yeah, but I think she went out the other door." She pointed down the hall, and Trace ran in that direction.

He couldn't see the door, and when he got closer, he heard a scuffle.

"Shut up!" a man's voice growled.

Trace went around the corner and his blood turned to ice in his veins. The man had his back to him, and he was standing near an exit, struggling to get Connie out the door.

"Hey!" Trace yelled and lunged for the guy. Rage thundered through him. All he could think about was getting the man away from Connie.

Trace wrapped his arms around the man's neck. Tightened. Squeezed. He dragged him backward until he released Connie. She fell to the floor.

Trace seethed with anger and spun the man around. He slammed his fist into David Atkinson's face and sent him staggering back. The man stumbled. Shook his head and righted himself. He glared at Trace with so much hatred that if his eyes had been weapons, Trace would be dead.

"I'm going to kill you!" Atkinson roared and charged.

He didn't get far. Trace grabbed the guy by the collar and slammed him to the floor. He pounced on him. Gripping his neck and holding him down, he punched

Atkinson in the face. He jabbed him again. Over and over and over until he drew blood.

"Trace! Trace!" He heard Connie screaming his name, but he couldn't stop. The thought of the man's hands on her made him even angrier, and he wanted to end David's miserable life. One punch after another, he wanted him to pay for terrorizing her.

"All right, all right. That's enough!" Someone grabbed Trace from behind and jerked him off of Atkinson.

Trace didn't give a damn about David; he looked around frantically for Connie. People were gathered everywhere, and though he heard her crying, he didn't see her.

"Connie!" he yelled and pushed past people until he saw her hurrying toward him. He lifted her, not thinking about whether she was hurt anywhere. He just needed to hold her.

"He was going to kill me," she cried, wrapping her arms in a death grip around his neck.

Her sobs came loud and hard, and her body shook violently. Trace held on. He fought his own tears as he buried his face into her hair. He could've lost her tonight.

"I love you. I love you so damn much. I thought…" He couldn't finish the statement. His chest tightened as he continued holding her. Knowing he could've lost her tonight scared him to death. "Baby, I'm never letting you go. Do you hear me? I'm never letting you go."

"Don't… Please…don't. I love you…"

Trace could barely make out her muffled words, but he heard what was most important. She loved him, too.

*A month later...*

"Oh, Trace. This is lovely," Connie said in awe when she stepped out on the patio of their beach villa. They were vacationing in the Bahamas, and it was their first day there.

The night air was warm and a little muggy as the waves crashed against the rocks, and a slight breeze kissed her heated cheeks. Connie always thought the balcony at his condo was the most peaceful place. But she had to admit, since being on vacation, their little slice of beach paradise was a close second.

She glanced around the patio, noting the areas that Trace had transformed. Clearly, he'd had help. Small twinkling lights had been hung on the side of the villa, just over the door and windows that faced the ocean. The table for two, covered in a white tablecloth with a large votive candle flickering in the middle, illuminated just enough for her to see the covered dishes. On the other side of the patio were two massage beds covered with white sheets. Soft jazz pierced the night, and Connie felt like she was in paradise.

"This is absolutely amazing."

"I figured we'd eat first," Trace said, pulling out a chair for her. "Then I have a couple of masseuses coming to give us a massage."

He claimed the seat across from her and poured two glasses of champagne.

"Shall we make a toast?" Connie asked, holding up her glass. They'd been through so much together in the last six weeks, she felt they could handle anything going forward.

"We're toasting to love, to perseverance and to happily-ever-afters. I love you, sweetheart, and I know we're going to have an incredible life together. Thank you for taking a chance on me."

"I love you more, and I appreciate you coming to my rescue and for being here for me every step of the way," she said and clinked her glass to his before they took a sip.

When Trace suggested they get away for a few days, Connie had had no idea that, with Trinity and Erica's help, he had already planned the trip. The itinerary covered ten days. The first seven days were just for the two of them to decompress, lie out on the beach and continue getting to know each other. They'd decided to slow down and get their relationship on track before thinking about marriage and a family. Connie had no doubt that they'd get there.

They were officially dating, and every day, she fell more and more in love with her man. Each day he did or said something that assured her that he was perfect for her, and that he would always protect her. She never knew it was possible to love someone so much and so completely until she'd met Trace.

The last three days of their trip would be spent with Trace's father and his father's girlfriend. Connie couldn't wait to meet the man who had raised four children as a single parent.

"Now, for dinner," Trace said, interrupting her thoughts.

With a wave of his arms, he dramatically removed the stainless-steel plate covers. "Ta-da!"

Connie stared at the table. French toast. Sausage. Hash browns. "Oh, Trace," she cooed, her hands on her chest. "I can't believe you remembered. Breakfast for dinner. My favorite."

"That's not all." He ran into their villa and returned with a plastic container.

Her mouth dropped open. "*No...* Those aren't your *to-die-for* cookies, are they?"

"They are," he said, grinning, and set the container on a cabinet next to the table.

"How? How did you do all of this? We haven't even been here twenty-four hours. And the cookies? I know you didn't have them when we first arrived."

"Never mind how—just dig in. Our masseuses will be here in forty-five minutes."

As Connie looked back over the last six weeks, so much of it seemed like a bad dream. The bank robbery and Richard's murder had started a snowball effect. Before she knew it, she'd been living a nightmare.

It had been like something out of a thriller novel, and Connie was glad it was over. It still blew her mind that the gray-eyed man, Daniel, the one she had seen at the bank, had an identical twin. She'd been shocked to learn that there were two of them, and the only difference in their appearance was that David, the model, didn't have any visible tattoos.

David was by far the evil twin, as far as Connie was concerned. During his interrogation, he had admitted to setting her house on fire and tracking her down the day before he confronted her at the theater. Knowing that she could've died at his hands was still unnerving. She didn't even want to think about what would've happened if Trace hadn't gotten to her in time.

Now that Daniel and David were behind bars, she could breathe easier. They were waiting to stand trial, and with all of the charges against them—robbery, murder and attempted murder, to name a few—it was safe to say that they'd be in jail for the rest of their lives.

Trace and Langston were officially in business together. After Trace resigned from LEPA, a couple of weeks later, Langston left the FBI. They were in talks with Trinity about building a partnership with LEPA and their own PI agency. Of course, she loved the idea, but had one stipulation for the guys—they both had to agree to fill in if ever she was short of security specialists. They agreed.

All of their lives were moving forward. Connie was still living in the safe house, but she and Trace were discussing moving in together. No time soon, but the idea was on the table.

"I guess the only thing missing is Vinnie Montell," Trace said with a straight face, then burst out laughing.

Connie shook her head and rolled her eyes. She couldn't understand why every time Vinnie's name came up Trace broke out laughing.

"From this day forward, *do not* mention his name," she said with mock disgust.

"Oh…" He sobered, but it was easy to see that he was fighting a smile. "What? Too soon?" Again, he lost it and stumbled out of his seat.

Connie couldn't hold back her own laughter. Despite all the bad things that had happened in the past weeks, and the losses she had endured, including Vinnie, something good had come of it all.

*Trace.*

He was the best thing that had ever happened to her. If it meant reliving the worst weeks of her life to have him…she'd do it all over again.

\* \* \* \* \*

## SPECIAL EXCERPT FROM

### ⒽHARLEQUIN
# ROMANTIC SUSPENSE

*When his nephew is taken, Jacob will do anything to
get him back, even if it means accidentally kidnapping
retrieval expert Norah Loblaw. Now they're working
together to get Desmond back—and trying to explain
their quickly growing feelings along the way.*

*Read on for a sneak preview of*
The Negotiator,
*Melinda Di Lorenzo's next thrilling romantic suspense!*

He thought she deserved the full truth.

*And I can't give it to her here and now.*

"It's a complicated situation," he stated, hearing how
weak that sounded even as he said it.

"Like Lockley?" Norah replied.

"She's a different animal completely."

The voices started up again, and Norah at last relented.

"Okay, I believe you need my help, and I'm willing to
hear you out," she said. "Let's go."

Jacob didn't let himself give in to the thick relief.
There was genuinely no time now. He spun on his heel
and led Norah back through the slightly rank parking lot.
When they reached his car, though, she stopped again.

"What are we doing?" she asked as he reached for the
door handle.

"I'd rather go over the details at my place. If you don't mind."

"You don't live here?" she asked, sounding confused.

"Here?" he echoed.

"I guess I just inferred…" She gave her head a small shake. "I'm guessing it's complicated? Again?"

He lifted his hat and scraped a hand over his hair. "You might say."

He gave the handle a tug, but Norah didn't move.

"Changing your mind?" he asked, his tone far lighter than his mind.

"No. But I need you to give me the keys," she said. "I want to drive. You can navigate."

"I thought you believed me."

"I believe you," she said mildly. "But that doesn't mean I come even close to trusting you."

Jacob nodded again, then held out the keys. As she took them, though, and he moved around to the passenger side, he realized that her words dug at him in a surprisingly forceful way. It wasn't that he didn't understand. He wouldn't have trusted himself, either, if the roles were reversed. Hell. It'd be a foolish move. It made perfect sense. But that didn't mean Jacob had to like it.